The Asian Billionaire's Forbidden Match

He's arranged to marry another, but he wants her...

A tantalizing romance, brought to you by best selling BWAM author Mary Peart!

Kimberly is the proud owner of Pet Haven, a pet daycare center. Happily single, she assumes it's going to stay that way... until she literally runs into the man of her dreams! Peter is a billionaire whose future is in a loveless arranged marriage.

When he meets Kimberly however, he's immediately smitten. Everything changes for both of them after that moment, and they start a forbidden romance. It doesn't take long for them to fall crazy in love; Peter knows that Kimberly is the woman he really wants to marry.

But with family pressures and Peter due to wed another in the near future, will his desires play a part in the choices he'll soon have to make? Find out in this emotional and gripping arranged marriage romance by best seller Mary Peart. Suitable for over 18s only due to sex scenes so hot, you'll be on the lookout for your own Asian billionaire.

Get Free Romance eBooks!

Hi there. As a special thank you for buying this book, for a limited time I want to send you some great ebooks completely **free of charge** directly to your email! You can get it by going to this page:

www.saucyromancebooks.com/physical

You can see a the cover of these books on the next page:

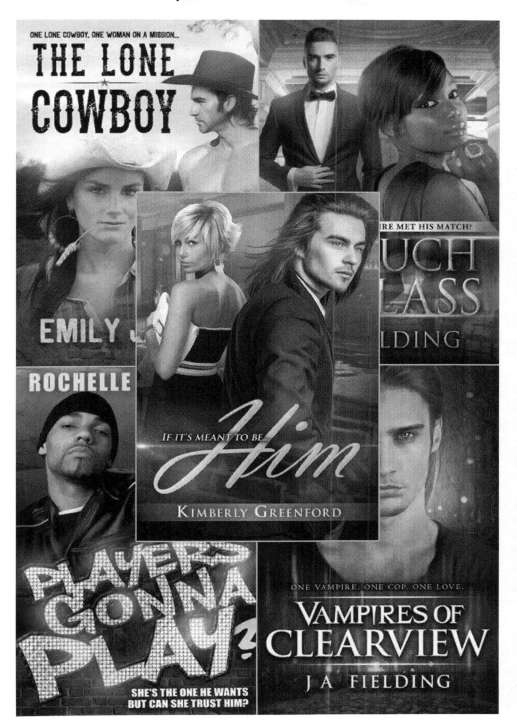

These ebooks are so exclusive you can't even buy them. When you download them I'll also send you updates when new books like this are available.

Again, that link is:

www.saucyromancebooks.com/physical

Contents

Chapter 1

"I don't see what the problem is, Deidre," Kimberly said impatiently as she tried to fit the key inside the lock to open the door to Pets Haven, the animal daycare she operated. "Dump him and stop expecting him to change, people rarely do." She pushed the door open and started opening the shutters and pulling the string to open the drapes. She opened at eight, but she always got there at seven-thirty for people who had to get to work early.

"I knew I should not have called you," her friend complained. "You are far too cynical and too hard on people. You don't understand, Kim, I love him, and he said he is trying, and what else can I do?"

"You are right." Kimberly dumped her pocket book on her desk and went to look around to see if Marjorie, the woman who came in to do the cleaning, had done a thorough job of emptying the water pans and the dishes she used to feed the animals from. She ran a very clean establishment and that was why she had so many clients because they got their money's worth. "I am not very tolerant because if it had been me I would have thrown his broke ass out a long time ago. But then again, you are not me, are you?"

"You just wait until you fall in love one day," the girl said with a sniff and hung up the phone.

Kimberly shrugged and went to the bathroom to take a look inside it. The place was small and homely, and she had acquired the lease quite by chance. After college, she had gone into teaching for a little bit but had seen how the high school kids behaved and had almost gotten her ass locked up because she had hauled a fifteen-year-old boy by his collar and told him that if he ever touched her ass again he was going to regret it. She had been called into a hearing by the principal, who told her that teaching was not for her. "You are right," she had told him right then and there. "I quit."

She had followed the family tradition because her mother and father had been teachers. Her mother still taught at the middle school and her father had taught right up until he had died of prostate cancer two years ago. She had told her mother that she did not have the stomach for it and she wanted to do something different. It helps that she was crazy about animals because as she had told her friends animals never betray you or pretend to be something they are not, the way people do.

She had been in business for a year now and was doing surprisingly well. She had hired a guy who came in from nine to four, and they got along well.

She went into one of the rooms to look at the stray dogs she had in cages. She also picked up neglected animals with the hope that people would adopt them and had been quite successful.

"Hey Cassie." She crouched down and ran her fingers through the thick luxurious fur of the mixed-breed dog she had found wandering around in her neighborhood. "How are you love?" Suddenly, there was a chorus of barking from the other five dogs there as they heard her voice. "Okay guys, quiet, I happen to be running a business here." She set about finding them some breakfast before going to the front to greet her first client for the day.

*****

"She told me she needs space, Kim. What should I make of it?" Brian Gamble asked her as he set about grooming the

Chihuahua's silky white fur. It was after eleven and all the cages were full with the animals that had been dropped off for them to take care of.

"It means she needs space, Brian, it's as simple as that." Kimberly looked at him in amusement. She had seen him come in to work in different emotional stages because of the same relationship; happy and carefree and blissfully in love one minute and the next with a hang-dog look because his girlfriend was not talking to him.

"Have you ever told a guy that?" he asked her anxiously, tying a pink bow at the top of the dog's head.

"Never been in a relationship long enough to tell any guy that," she reminded him. He had always been amazed that a 'fine looking' girl like her was still single and had never been in a proper relationship. At one point, he had asked her bluntly if she was gay. "Why, because I do not choose to be with a man just for the very reason of showing the world that I have one?" She had laughed at him, her beautiful white teeth flashing and lighting up her oval-shaped face. "I want someone who is going to rock my world or not at all."

"Oh, I keep forgetting." Brian looked at his young employer curiously. She was small and curvaceous and had the most beautiful cocoa-brown skin he had ever seen and large dark eyes. She had thick black hair that she wore natural, mostly twisted into a knot on top of her head. "You want someone who is going to rock your world. What if that does not happen?"

"Then I am content to stay this way. I am happy being single, Brian, and maybe you should consider that for a little bit. Your relationship is making you very unhappy and there comes a time when you have to ask yourself if it is really worth it."

*****

The Kamato's household was not very impressive from the outside. Red brick smoothed away by the elements and sparkling glass doors and windows. It was a two-story building with five bedrooms and four baths and a wraparound porch. There was plenty of yard space, and at this time of the year, the garden was rioting with colors from the variety of flowers planted.

John Kamato and his wife, Mitsu Kamato, had come over from Japan when they were only teenagers and had married each other in a simple ceremony planned by both their parents. It was an arranged marriage and even though they were not in love, they had grown to appreciate and respect each other. It was a tradition for them and they knew nothing else. John Kamato had started working in his father's supermarket and over the years had worked hard and saved until by the time he was twenty-five years old he had acquired a chain of supermarkets around the country. In his late thirties, he had added department stores to the list and had become a billionaire over the years. They had one son, Peter, who was being groomed and a nice Japanese girl had been picked out for him to marry.

They were not big on showing emotions and Peter had never seen his parents hold hands. He knew they shared separate bedrooms and had come to think of it as being natural. He was given the best of everything and had been sent to the best business school in order to capably run the business and had been sitting on the board since he had graduated from Harvard where he had done his masters in business. He had worked in the company since he had been going to high school and although he was the 'boss's son,' he had not been given special privileges but had been required to pack groceries until he had moved up in the ranks. He was now senior vice president at Kamato's Holdings.

He had met his intended bride sometime last week when she and her parents had come over for a visit and had had dinner with them. She was being groomed to be his wife, and for the entire time during dinner she had kept her eyes downcast, only speaking in monosyllables when he spoke to her. She was very attractive and would make a very good wife, but Peter found himself wishing that he could have a conversation with her. Her parents owned several toy stores and they were going to be giving them two of the stores when they got married. For some reason, he was not looking forward to being married to her.

*****

Mitsui Kamato rubbed the expensive cream on her skin slowly sitting in front of the large vanity mirror on her dresser. She had noticed several wrinkles at the sides of her eyes and was determined to get rid of them. She was not vain, but she hated imperfection of any kind and had the creams and vials to prove it. She brushed her long curtain of black waist-length hair vigorously making sure the strokes were even. She loved the arrangement of being in the room by herself and did not mind it one bit that her husband was halfway across the corridor in his own suite of rooms. They had never been in love and at this point they never would be and she had accepted that. What they had was better than love. The emotion tended to fade and leave scars but what they had would continue for the long haul and besides she had her secret and the arrangement suited her quite fine!

*****

"Hi mom! I thought you had some sort of a staff meeting or the other," Kimberly said in surprise as her mother came through towards her tiny office. Karen Gayle was in her mid-fifties but her small frame looked more like forty instead. Apart from being a very good English Language teacher, she was also a mentor for young people who lacked direction. Kimberly looked like her in every way except her personality. Karen was gentle and tolerant while Kimberly was like a fierce lion protecting her cubs and did not suffer fools gladly.

"It got cancelled so I decided to come and visit my daughter whom I have not seen in a week," she said mildly, putting down her pocketbook and her extra bag on a table nearby.

The weather had turned out to be nice for August and she was wearing a thin cotton dress with a jacket over it.

"You are not going to make me feel guilty for not coming over, are you?" Kimberly raised one thick brow. She had been buried in paperwork since two o'clock and had made sure Brian could manage by himself before doing the dreaded task.

"Of course not, I am hoping that you will accomplish that all by yourself," her mother said with a teasing smile. "I picked up some food for you as well. When was the last time you went grocery shopping?"

"I think I went last week." Kimberly tapped the pen against her cheek thoughtfully. "Oh wait! I just picked up some milk and eggs. Mom, you know I hardly ever use my kitchen."

"I know," her mother said with a sigh, taking out a sandwich and a bottle of iced tea. "I figured you have not eaten yet since this morning."

"Thanks, Mom, you are the best," Kimberly said gratefully, reaching for the food. After her father had died, she had contemplated going back home to stay with her mother, but she had firmly told her that she would be fine.

"So how are you?" Karen asked her daughter. She had often wondered where her fierce spirit had come from but as her husband had laughingly told her: "I am sure she got that from your mother, dear."

"I am fine. Just a little bit concerned about Cassie," she said referring to the pup she had found a few weeks ago. "I have a feeling she has become very attached to me. I wish I could take her, Mom, but who is going to take care of her?"

"You could keep her right here and take her home with you when you leave," Karen suggested.

"On my bike?" Kimberly asked in amusement. "I don't think that would work."

*****

John Kamato was a smart man and he had had to be in order to be in the business he was in. He ran his company and his home like a tight ship and he did not let emotions get in the way. He had a son to carry on the business and he had made sure to train him well and he had seen the boy improving as the time went by and he knew he was ready to take over from him. He had no intention of leaving entirely, he was used to working and being in charge so much and for so long that he did not know how to stay still.

He glanced at the figures on his desk with a frown and made a call. "Tell my son I need a meeting with him sometime today," he murmured briefly to his secretary.

*****

"I am sure she is going to be okay, Mrs. Mitchell. Have you taken her to see the vet?" The poor woman was almost beside herself with worry. She had several cats and they were her only companions since her husband had passed away ten years ago, and whenever she was going to do her shopping or go to play bridge with her friends, she always left them at the daycare.

"He said it's just colic, but my poor baby is not eating. How was she today?"

"She ate a little bit and had some water and slept most of the time," Kimberly advised her. It was past closing time, but she never rushed her customers, preferring to hear whatever they had to say before they left, no matter the hour.

"Do you think I should take her back?"

"Why don't you watch her for a day or two and then if she does not improve then you take her back?" Kimberly suggested.

"All right, dear, I will do so." Mrs. Mitchell folded a twenty dollar note in her palm as she was leaving. No matter how much Kimberly protested that she was paid enough, the woman always left a tip for her whenever she was leaving along with her check. "You are such a beautiful young lady and so kind and thoughtful, just buy yourself something nice with it."

Brian had already gone home, so she checked that the dogs left there were okay and spent a little time with Cassie before locking up and securing the place.

She slide on her helmet and loosened the chain around her bike in readiness to go home. The weather had gotten milder now that it was coming down to the end of August and there was a slight breeze fanning her skin as she made her way home. She always took the scenic route and sometimes stopped at the park to feed the ducks. School was still out for the summer and she saw children with their parents sitting on the benches enjoying a late picnic or feeding the ducks. She was in no hurry to get home and sometimes she stopped to buy pizza or Italian food at the restaurant a few blocks from where she lived.

"The usual?" Leonardo, the owner, asked her with a smile on his ruddy and jovial face.

"You know me so well, Leo," she told him with a grin as he passed her the delicious smelling pasta and meat balls already packaged.

*****

She took a shower and pulled an old t-shirt over her head before unwrapping her thick black hair and braiding it and putting the braids together to secure them with a rubber band before padding into the kitchen with bare feet to sit at the counter and enjoy her meal with a glass of red wine. She loved living alone and her friends could not understand how she could stand to be in the tiny apartment all by herself most of the time. "That's because I enjoy my own company," she had told them firmly. "You should try it sometimes."

Her phone rang just as she was about to wash out her glass. "I hope you are not about to tell me you were in bed, unless it's with a perfectly hot and muscular body beside you," her friend from college, Simone Bailey, said in amusement. She, Deidre, and Simone got together at least one time a week to chat about what was happening in their lives. Simone was a teacher as well and had been away to Tuscany for the holiday.

"You are back?" Kimberly said with a delighted squeal.

"I got back yesterday to get ready for school and you would never believe it! I met someone there. Lord, Kimmie! I cannot believe that I had to go so many thousands of miles to meet a guy."

"You left him there?" Kimberly asked in amusement.

"He is a wine grower and has a small farm. I spent the entire six weeks helping him and making love from dusk till dawn. It was orgasmic," Simone said with a blissful sigh. They had been called the three musketeers in college and were as different as night and day. Deidre was tall and skinny with short cropped black spiky hair and eyes too large for her face while Kimberly was petite and curvaceous and stunningly beautiful. Simone, on the other hand, was a redhead with startling green eyes and very white skin that she tried to tan without success over the years. They had the ability to turn heads wherever they went.

"So what now?"

"He is coming here in December and we are going to take it from there," Simone told her. "I could hardly bear to tear myself out of his arms when I had to leave."

"You should have stayed."

"I thought about that myself, but I have to be sure. Kimmie, you are the one who is always telling me to make sure it's right before I make a total commitment," she reminded her.

"Who am I to give relationship advice?" Kimberly said with a little laugh, pouring herself another glass of wine and taking it into the living room. "Deidre is mad at me right now because I told her to dump the loser she is living with."

"Oh jeez, Kimmie, way to be diplomatic," Simone said in exasperation. "You cannot tell a woman who fancies herself in love to just go cold turkey like that. Telling her to dump him will only fuel her desire to want him more."

"That's why I am not in a relationship. Too many rules," Kimberly said wryly. "Now about the Italian hottie…"

*****

That night she pondered the conversation she had with her friend and wondered about her lack of a relationship. She had ventured into one while she had been in college and it had turned out that he had been seeing several other women on campus as well. It had been no great loss because her heart had not been in it. She had sworn from then that she had to be totally and completely in love with the man to give him her body and she was not going to accept anything less.

Her mother and father had been in love with each other until the day he died and she had always admired how they managed to laugh with each other and be happy together and had decided that she wanted something like what they had shared.

*****

Her name was Natsuko, and of course Peter wanted to get to know her better before they joined together as man and wife. He had told her that they should go out to dinner without their parents being there and she had looked at him as if he had asked her to strip naked and dance on top of the table. "We can't," she had muttered in a whisper, holding her head down in case she had offended him. She was very pretty with soft doe-like eyes and raven hair that hung down to her waist. She was always just in a kimono the few times he had seen her and he wondered if that was all that was in her wardrobe. She had been born in America just like him but had obviously not adopted the lifestyle the way he had.

He stifled his impatience. They were sitting in the living room while their parents enjoyed after-dinner drinks in the dining room. His father had suggested that they go into the room and try to get to know each other better. "I just want to get to know you, Natsuko, after all we are going to be married soon."

"As you wish," she bowed her head formally and that was the end of the conversation. It was going to be a long hard marriage!

Chapter 2

It was raining and hard too! An end-of-summer shower the weather guy had put it when she listened to the report this morning. She always rode her bike whether rain or shine, sunshine or snow because she considered herself helping the environment and it was good exercise as well. She put on a knee-length raincoat over her denims and blue dress shirt and donned a pair of matching rain boots as well. She had put her regular shoes in her backpack and headed towards the door.

It happened when she was near to work. Trying to race the cab that was about to douse her with water, she did not see him crossing the street and crashed right into him taking both of them to the hard pavement. She fell on top of him and heard his groan before rolling off quickly and getting to her feet. "Jeez, I am so sorry." She looked down at him and reached out her hand to help him up hoping he was not very hurt. "Are you okay?"

He stood up and brushed off his very nice and expensive looking suit, giving her a narrowed look. "Do you always ride like that?" His voice was deep and very cultured and judging from the black hair plastered to his skull and his slanted eyes, she knew he was of Asian descent.

"I was trying to beat the cab and stop it from drowning me with the water," she said, apologizing again. "My store is right over there, how about you get cleaned up?"

He hesitated briefly and then nodded, walking beside her as they made their way to Pets Haven. She had taken off her helmet and looped it around the handle of her bike and fished her keys out of her backpack, quickly opening the door. She hesitated briefly as she realized that she was going to let a perfect stranger inside and she was going to be alone for a couple of hours. It did not excuse the fact that he was well dressed. Serial killers and rapists came in all forms and shapes and expensive wear.

Ah well the damage was done already, she thought as she gestured for him to come inside while she opened the shutters and the windows. "I'll go get a towel," she said hurrying off into the bathroom, coming out quickly in case he had followed her. She handed him the towel and took off her dripping raincoat, hanging it on the coat hanger. "Quite a weather we are having, huh?" she asked more for something to say. He looked like he did not talk much.

He nodded and handed her back the towel.

"Would you like a cup of coffee?" she asked him quickly.

Once again the hesitation, and then he nodded.

What a talker, she thought sarcastically as she went to put the coffee pot on.

"What is this place?" he asked her, looking around.

"It's a day care center for pets," she told him, pulling off her rain boots and taking out her flats from her bag and putting them on. "We also have stray animals in case you were thinking of adopting."

He looked at her with a trickle of amusement. "No, thank you. I am not much of an animal person."

"I am." She hurried into the little alcove to pour the coffee into two ceramic cups. "How do you take it?"

"Black without sugar."

"Very brave of you. I love tons of heavy cream and a little sugar and cinnamon." She came back with the coffee and handed him his. "My name is Kimberly Gayle and I am the owner of this fine establishment."

"Peter Kamato," he said with a brief nod.

"Is that Japanese?" she asked him curiously.

"Yes. I was born here, but my parents are from Japan," he said briefly. "Do you actually make a living doing this?"

"What you think I just open the place up because I have nothing else to do?" she asked him mildly.

He looked at her in surprise as if he was not accustomed to being talked to that way. "No, I am sorry. It just seems to be a strange way to make a living."

"And what do you do, Mr. Peter Kamato? Work in some executive office and tell people where to go and what to do?" she asked him coolly, looking him over.

"Something like that." He was fascinated by her boldness and her frank manner; no one had ever had such a total disregard of him before.

"I make a very good living from this and moreover I enjoy animals better than people so it's perfect." She put her cup on the table. "Are you sure you are okay?"

"I am sure. I will require your number if I go home later and start feeling pain or the need to go to the hospital," he told her mock seriously.

"Not a chance," she said with a careless smile. "You can always send one of your minions to get me."

"I will come and get you myself," he assured her, standing up and stretching out a hand. "Very nice bumping into you, Ms. Gayle."

"It's Kimberly," she told him with a smile, taking his hand in hers. He held on a little longer than necessary before letting go.

"Well, I will be going. Thanks for the coffee." With a brief nod, he headed for the door.

"If you change your mind about the dog, please let me know," she called out to him as he reached the door.

He stopped and turned to look at her, his dark eyes unreadable as he stared at her. "I doubt it," he said with a slow smile before leaving.

*****

"I almost drowned out there!" Brian rushed inside and closed his oversized umbrella, shaking his spiky brown hair much like a dog shaking water off his fur. "I cannot believe this weather. I need a strong cup of coffee and a doughnut before I can start working. I definitely need a sugar rush this morning." He took off his raincoat and hung it on the coat hanger next to hers and went straight to the still hot coffee pot. "You had company?" he asked her, curiously eyeing the two coffee mugs.

She told him about the incident this morning.

"How did he look?" Brian asked filling his cup to the brim and pouring milk inside it while reaching for a sugary doughnut.

"What?" Kimberly looked at him with a little frown.

"Was he handsome or one of those run-of-the-mill Asian guys with broad face and little else?"

"You are unbelievable," Kimberly said in disgust, heading towards the cages to feed the dogs. Even though it was pouring down rain, people still had to get to work so there would still be people coming in.

The rain eased up within the next hour, and they were kept busy with the animals for the next three hours. Their best customer, Millie, wanted them to groom and take her pooches out for a walk for an hour to get their regular exercise. The large bottled-blonde woman was married to a millionaire and fancied herself one of the elites of society and tried to behave as such. At one point, Brian had baulked at her ridiculous request, but Kimberly had told him that she was a customer and whatever she wanted done, as long as it was nothing out of the way, then they were going to be doing it.

So she took them out for a walk in the park and sat on one of the benches while they frolicked around before taking them back.

Her job was very interesting.

*****

Peter took off the slightly wet jacket and hung it up on the hanger inside his office. He still felt slightly sore from the fall but otherwise he felt his mood lighten. He had not been looking because he had been glancing at his watch as he was running late for a meeting. He had been about to reprimand the person, but she had taken off her helmet and he had gotten a good look at her. Instead of looking bedraggled and the worse for wear, she looked like a water nymph or a sea sprite. Then they had gone inside her little store and she had taken off her rain jacket and he had gotten a good look at her. He sat behind his desk and pictured her handing him his cup of coffee and telling him about adopting a pet. She had made him forget where he was and who he was for just that time and he realized that he wanted to see her again!

*****

He went into the store the day after. He had a meeting across town, near to where the store was, and when the meeting had ended, he had sent the driver along and told him he had another stop to make so he would give him a call. It was the first day of September and the rain had abated somewhat and the place looked new and washed clean. He stood across the street and looked at the building. It was a quaint little place and he was surprised he had not noticed it before. The mid morning traffic had slowed down and he crossed the street, remembering her running into him just two days ago.

He pushed the door open and went inside. He did not see her at first and then he did. She was crouched beside a basket that had a small dog inside it and she was saying something to the animal. A young man came over to him and asked him politely if he could be of help. "I am here to see, Ms. Gayle."

She looked up as soon as she heard her name and came towards him. "It's okay, Brian, I will take it from here."

"So, you came," she said with an engaging smile leading him towards her small office, knowing that Brian's inquisitive gaze would be on them. "Either you are here to adopt an animal or you found out you have internal bleeding and you here to tap me for some cash."

"How much do you have?" he asked her teasingly, surprising himself by asking.

She gestured for him to take a seat on one of the chairs in front of her desk. "Let's see?" She pretended to think about it.

"Considering that your suit costs more than I make in one year, I would say not enough."

He looked at her for a spell. She was truly beautiful. Her hair was twisted into an elaborate style at the side of her neck and she was wearing some sort of green sparkling earrings that almost touched her shoulders. It matched the blouse she was wearing and her faded denim hugged her curves like a glove. "In that case, I would have to let it go." His lips curved into a smile. "I was just in the neighborhood and decided to stop by and say hello."

"Were you really in the neighborhood?" she asked him curiously. "People usually say that, but it is far from being the truth."

"I was," he told her and then told her the name of the company.

"So you are really telling the truth," she teased him.

"I am." He hesitated briefly. "Would you like to have dinner with me?" he asked, surprising them both.

"Dinner." She sat back and looked at him curiously. "Actually, my mother told me never to go out with strangers, but considering I almost killed you with my bike, I supposed we are well acquainted." Her eyes were laughing at him.

"So, the answer is yes?" he asked with bated breath.

"I suppose it is. I never turn down a meal because I hate to cook," she told him unabashedly.

"Is that so?" He looked at her in amusement.

"Absolutely," she answered. Just then her phone rang. "Excuse me," she said and answered the call. "Yes, Mrs. Mitchell, of course I understand. Don't worry about it, your babies will be quite okay and I will make sure to give them the medicine. Of course. No thanks necessary."

He had been watching her as she spoke on the phone and noticed her small hands drumming on the desk as she spoke to the person.

"One of my very fussy clients," she told him with a smile. "So, where were we?"

"Making plans for dinner."

*****

"He is a handsome one," Brian murmured as soon as Peter had left the store.

"Who?" Kimberly asked innocently as she put the spoon inside the cat's mouth to give him the dosage recommended.

"You know who," Brian said impatiently. "Is he the one you almost creamed with your bike?"

"Yes," she answered briefly, checking to see if the others were okay.

"And he came back why?" Brian persisted and Kimberly sighed as she went to get herself a cup of coffee.

"None of your business," she told him firmly.

*****

"I have dinner plans," Kimberly told her friends. They were on speaker phone while she rummaged inside her closet to try and find something suitable to wear. She was going out with a man she barely knew and she did not feel the usual reservations about doing so.

"With who?" Deidre demanded.

"Whom," Kimberly said absently as she examined a black wool dress she had not worn in ages. Was it too sexy, she wondered looking at the deep plunging neckline and remembering that it hugged her figure very close.

"So, you are giving me grammar lessons now?" Deidre asked her friend.

"Aren't I always?" Kimberly asked teasingly. "Listen guys, it's no big deal, it's just this guy I bumped into and I mean that literally, and he came by two days ago to ask me out to dinner. He is Japanese."

"You are going out with a Japanese guy?" Simone asked her, the tone skeptical.

"I am having dinner with him," Kimberly corrected her, deciding to wear the dress after all. "You are making it out to be something more than it is."

"When was the last time you had dinner with a guy?" Simone asked her.

"I cannot remember," she said impatiently. "You were the ones encouraging me to go out and now I am going and you have a problem with it."

"What does he do?" Simone asked suspiciously.

"I have not asked him because, as I said before, this is not a relationship, we are just going out."

*****

They had dinner at a fancy French restaurant downtown. He had picked her up at home in a black sports car. "Midlife crisis comes early for you?" she teased him as he opened the door for her. She shivered a little as the cold air nipped at her cheeks. She had put on a black jacket over her dress and pulled it close to her.

"I love cars, fast ones. It's one of my vices." He slid behind the wheel and shoved the stick into gear causing the car to purr like a well-oiled machine.

"I don't much go for cars, too much pollutants and I am leaning towards green." He was wearing a dark-blue dress pants and black-and-white sweater. His raven-black hair was combed back from his forehead and his jaw was freshly shaven.

"Is that why you ride a bike?" He glanced at her briefly. When she had opened the door for him when he arrived, he had been pole axed when he had seen her. The dress against her skin and the plunging neckline showing glimpses of her curves.

"Mostly and for the exercise aspect of it too, I don't get to do that much so improvise."

*****

"So, what do you do?" She examined the coq au vin and tasted it tentatively. "I have not tried French cuisine much," she told him. "This is very good," she decided.

"I am glad you like it," he told her in amusement. "I am in a management position at a holding company."

"Do you enjoy being in the corporate world?" she asked him curiously.

"I do." He nodded, realizing that although he had not lied to her, he had not exactly told her the truth and he knew why. "It's very fascinating."

"Holding company? It means that the company has other businesses under its umbrella right?"

"It does. What about you? You always knew you wanted to run an animal daycare?"

She laughed softly and his eyes were riveted to her lips. She was wearing a nude-colored lip gloss, but the shine brought attention to her full lips. "I was a school teacher for two years before I decided it was definitely not for me."

He looked at her in surprise. "What happened?"

She told him about the incident that had gotten her going to the principal's office and she had decided there and then that teaching was definitely not for her.

"You are not much for rules are you?" He looked at her contemplatively. Their dinner plates had been removed and they were having crepe Suzettes.

"Not very," She sipped the wine appreciatively. "My mom and dad were always despairing of me whenever I went anywhere because I always argued my way out of something I did not think was right. That's why I had to open my own business."

"What if you had no choice but to follow tradition?" he asked her seriously.

Kimberly looked at him knowing that he was waiting for the answer and it would mean something to him. She had just met him, but for the first time she felt a rapport with someone of the opposite sex. "There is always a choice," she told him slowly. "Traditions are a part of our lives, but sometimes we need to make our own instead of following someone else's."

He swirled the rest of the liquid inside his glass, his expression brooding. "You are right," he told her quietly. Then with a smile, he changed the subject.

*****

Peter sat in the darkened room with the clothes he had worn to dinner still on. He had taken her home like a gentleman and shook her hand, telling her that he had enjoyed the evening and told her he would call her and then he left.

He had driven home with the silence in the car magnifying his thoughts. He had come home and used the side doors to go up to his suite. He had contemplated moving out several times, but he knew his parents would not approve. They had told him that they would give them an apartment for their wedding gift. He was all set to get everything he had worked so hard for and he did not want to give it up. He knew his father would not be adverse to him having a mistress and with the way his intended bride was behaving, it was something he was probably going to have to do.

He had enjoyed Kimberly's company and had been drawn to her from the moment she had bumped into him with her bike. He was not supposed to have gone out that morning but had decided to go and get a pretzel on the side of the road like he did sometimes. If he had not gone out that morning, he would not have met her and he would be going into his loveless marriage with no regrets. Now he was having second thoughts!

*****

Kimberly undressed slowly, hanging up her dress carefully and putting it away in the closet. She had had fun and she never thought she would have, but she had enjoyed herself. He was okay even though she was not thinking of a relationship because heck, she did not know the guy! But she definitely felt comfortable with him. He was obviously wealthy because of the clothes he wore and the car he drove, but that did not mean anything to her, she liked him and that was that!

*****

Hs mother was standing at her bedroom window looking when she saw his car drive in. He had told them that he was not going to make dinner and that he had something to do, but she had seen him rush home and shower and chang and go back out. He looked definitely like he had a date. She had never been able to relate to him, the son she had borne and nursed for several months before passing him to a nanny to do the bringing up. She had been happy that she had never been able to have more children and besides that would mean having sex with her husband and he did not much enjoy doing so with her. She never enjoyed it either and had endured it because it was her duty. When he had stopped doing so and left her alone, it had been the happiest time of her life!

Chapter 3

He had to see her again! It had been two weeks since they had dinner and he had been weighing the odds and consequences of pursuing this and had tried to reason with himself about what he was going into, but no amount of logic could sway him from the fact that he wanted to see her again. He had not called her, but he thought about her constantly. He never thought about his intended bride at all only when she was at the house for dinner, but here he was thinking about this girl he had just met.

He frowned into his coffee cup and tapped his hands on the desk. He had come in early to deal with the paperwork for a supermarket they had acquired and he could not concentrate on the documents before him. He glanced at the clock on his desk and realized that it was seven-thirty. He knew she always went to work early as she had told him that. With a sudden decision, he reached for his cell phone and dialed her number.

"Hello?" Her voice was a little breathless and he could just imagine her racing from one end of the room to answer the phone.

"You sound like you were running a marathon," he said softly.

"Peter?"

"Were you expecting someone else?"

"I was actually. I am expecting a call from the President of the United States," she said facetiously. "If his call comes in, I am going to have to hang up on you."

He laughed! Ever since he had met her and being around her, he found that he had fun and he could free up himself. "Duly noted. How are you?"

"I am okay. How goes it in the corporate world?"

"As well as can be." He paused. "I want to see you again."

She did not hesitate or play coy as some women would do. "I want to see you again too. How about dinner at my place?"

"I thought you did not cook?" he asked in amusement.

"There is such a thing as take-out and it happens to be my best friend," she told him gaily.

"Friday night works for you?"

"Yes. I will close up at seven and it will take me half hour to get home, so eight is good."

"I'll bring the wine."

*****

"I think I like him," Kimberly admitted. She and her friends were having lunch at the pizza place near to the store. Deidre worked as a legal secretary for the law firm downtown and Simone had taken her lunch break to coincide with theirs. Kimberly had left Brian to tend to the animals, making sure that everything was okay. "I have never felt so comfortable with someone of the opposite sex before."

"What do you know about him?" Simone asked her, squeezing the excess oil from her slice of pizza. She was dressed in a green pants suit and her glorious red hair was in a ponytail and bounced each time she moved her head. Deidre was dressed in a chic charcoal-grey suit with a light-blue blouse and Kimberly had on a dark blue dress pants and white blouse. Her hair had been braided and the plaits wrapped in a neat chignon. She had on powder-blue dangling earrings and light makeup. They were attracting a lot of attention from the opposite sex who had come in for lunch.

"I know he is in corporate and he wears expensive clothes." Kimberly grinned, digging into her salad. "I just know that I like him, okay? It's not a relationship really, we are just having fun together."

"You do not know anything about the guy and you claim you are having fun with him. You have never been into a real relationship in your life. Do you actually know what you are doing?" Simone asked her.

"You are making a big deal out of this," Kimberly protested, drinking her water. "We are just having fun."

*****

Mitsu Kamato sighed contentedly and settled back in the lounge chair. The day was beautiful and she had taken the chance to be with him. She had met Charles Baker during one of her trips to jazz classes. He had come in there looking out of place and their instructor had paired them together. They had hit it off immediately. He was a piano teacher and had lessons at his home. He was a widower without children and spent his time giving lessons and taking all sorts of classes.

"I took a cooking class at the community center just two weeks ago," he said, his light-blue eyes twinkling as he looked down at her. He was tall and stately and had been in the Army when he was younger. "I learned how to cook breaded chicken and wild rice."

"That's all?" she had asked him curiously, feeling herself relax underneath his arms. She was comfortable with him and she had just met him. The way she had never been comfortable with her own husband after thirty years of marriage.

"I also learned to bake carrot cake and chocolate cookies," he said with a laugh. He had a full head of dark hair liberally streaked with grey.

That was four months ago and they had met for coffee at a way-out coffee house and she had told him about her marriage.

"John and I have an arrangement that worked for the years we have been together." She stirred the coffee with cinnamon stick. "I never thought to question it because it was a tradition that had been in our family for generations."

"What about love?" he had asked her gently.

"Love tends to fade." She looked up at him and felt the spark that she had been feeling since she first met him. She had never cheated on her husband even though she knew he had casual sex with women, which had never mattered to her. "What we have will last for a life time."

"You have been fed that line all your life so that you started to believe it," he told her gravely. "I was married to Sophia since we were both in our early twenties and it was a love match. We had our differences, but we were committed to each other and that remained until she was taken from me. The only regret was that we never had children."

"Tell me some of the things you did together," she asked him.

He looked at her for a moment as if sensing if she really wanted to know what she had been missing. "We traveled to different places. She was a school teacher and we would scrimp and save for the times when she was on holidays from school and we would go to Europe or the Caribbean or even go to other states but we always try to get away and we never take each other for granted." He stared across the room wistfully and Mitsui felt her heart as she saw the expression of love on his face. She never had that and she knew now she wanted it.

"That sounds good," she said faintly, staring down at her rapidly cooling cup of coffee. "I travel sometimes but alone." She smiled. "John was always too busy to go with me even though he goes away for business."

He leaned forward and took her slender hands in his large ones. "I loved Sophia and I loved the life we had together as short as it was. I have learned one very important thing in the marriage and in life; the time is too short for us to be in something where we are unhappy. You are the first woman I have ever met since Sophia died that I have ever felt drawn to and I have never thought about being with someone who is married. I am attracted to you and I have been trying to fight it being the gentleman I am." He smiled at her. "I am not sure I want to fight it anymore.

"Neither am I." She lifted her gaze and looked at him. "I am not going to fight it anymore."

So, now they were at his house and he had cooked for her. She had left her house at a quarter to six because on Thursdays her husband went to his club and did not come home until midnight, so she met him every Thursday. "You made pasta. Are you still taking lessons?"

"I knew how to cook this from a long way back," he told her with a grin as he placed the meal before her. He knew how much money her husband had and made it a point of duty not to talk about him when they were together. "How is the wine?" He took a seat beside her.

"Lovely," she told him with a smile as she sipped it. They had been meeting together for the past four months now and he had never touched her but had kissed her softly on the mouth one night when she was leaving. She had felt her pulse quicken and her arms tighten around his waist wanting him to deepen the kiss, but he had pulled away from her.

"I wish I could stay here with you," she told him wistfully.

"I don't want to do it this way, Mitsu, we need to take our time and go slow," he told her gently. "In the meantime, let's enjoy this meal that I spent so much time making perfect," he said with a grin.

*****

"Right on time," she said with a smile as she let him in. "And you brought me flowers and wine."

He hung up his coat on the hanger and gave her the flowers he had brought her. She sniffed them in appreciation and went to put them in a glass vase of water. "I am going to pour the wine." She hurried into the kitchen and grabbed two wine glasses.

"How have you been?" he asked her formally. He wanted to touch her, but he had to restrain himself. She was wearing a short denim skirt and short white sweater and was not wearing any shoes. Dark-blue earrings dangled at her lobes and her hair was caught up in a jeweled clip at the nape of her neck.

"Really?" She looked at him with raised brow. His dark hair had blown on his forehead and he looked dark and formally handsome in his black sweater and black denims. "You sound as if you are meeting me for the first time. Come on, let's go and get drunk." She took his hand and led him towards the sofa. He felt his pulse jumping at her touch and the desire uncurled inside him.

She sat with her feet curled underneath her and sipped the wine. "I spent the day walking a dog with more energy than I had and when I came back to the store I could not function for several minutes."

"It keeps you fit as well?" he said lightly, watching the way her face lit up as she told her story and knew that he had to kiss her.

"I never thought of that." She stretched languidly. "How about dinner?"

"I am not hungry," he told her abruptly. "I have been struggling with something."

"What is it?" she asked him curiously.

"I have tried to tell myself that I should not be doing this but I cannot stop myself." He came and joined her on the sofa. "I am attracted to you."

"So, what's wrong with that?" she asked him, softly uncurling her feet from under her.

"I don't know." He touched her cheek softly. "I knew the day you charged into me that I was in big trouble." He laughed shortly. "I never knew how much." He pulled her onto his lap and framed her face with his hands. "You are so damned beautiful." He bent his head and took her lips with his slowly. Kimberly opened her mouth beneath his and looped her hands around his neck, sinking into the kiss. Her heart pounded inside her breasts and she felt her body growing warm from the fire within and her nipples stiffened as he deepened the kiss.

He felt himself tightened and the erection pressed against her bottom as the desire floated between them. She had been kissed before but never like this! She pressed against his body knowing that she wanted more. Before she could transmit her needs to him he dragged his mouth away from hers, his breathing ragged. He put her away from him and stood up drunkenly, his dark eyes narrowed as he stared down at her. "I can't stay," he said abruptly.

"Why not?" she demanded, her awakened body shivering from the need inside her.

"I need air," he told her and headed for the door. Kimberly jumped off the sofa and stopped him before he reached the door. He had already put on his coat and she knew he was getting ready to leave.

"What is going on, Peter?" she asked him, coming between him and the door.

"I just need to go." He stood there staring down at her, not daring to touch her. "I am sorry, this was a mistake."

"You are going to have to do better than that," she told him coolly, planting her hands on her hips. She looked like a small tornado with her eyes flashing and her bosom heaving. "I am not some teenager or inept woman who is going to swallow that, so try again."

"I want you," he told her tightly.

"So have me," she told him softly, pushing her hands inside his sweater and feeling his skin against the thin white shirt he had underneath.

"No" he whispered achingly, reaching down to pull her against him. "You don't know what you are doing." He took her lips with his hungrily, pressing her back against the door, one hand around her throat. His tongue ravaged hers and

Kimberly clung to him feverishly as she felt the desire flooding her body.

With a groan, he lifted the sweater over her head and realized that she was not wearing a bra. Her breasts were very generous for her size, the nipples a dusky brown that had stiffened from desire. He bent his head and took her nipple inside his mouth, pulling it and using his tongue massage it. Kimberly gasped and threw back her head, her body on fire! She shoved her fingers through his soft dark hair and moaned softly, feverishly as he moved over to the next one. "Peter," she muttered, wanting him to go further. He released her nipple and straightened up to look at her. She was unashamed of her body and leaned back against the door as he looked at her, his eyes narrowed, his body shaking. She was beautiful! With a tortured groan, he let her go. "I have to go," he told her, his expression tortured. "Please don't ask me why."

She moved away from the door and allowed him to leave, her body shivering and frustrated with need.

*****

www.SaucyRomanceBooks.com/RomanceBooks

Peter rested his head against the steering wheel as soon as he got into his vehicle. He had not meant to touch her, but he had not been able to help himself. He was drawn to her like a magnet drawn to steel and when she had suggested they had dinner at her home he should have said no and gone to somewhere public. He had thought he could control himself around her. He was very good at not letting his emotions control him, but he had underestimated the power she was beginning to have over him.

He turned on the engine and drove away, his thoughts troubled. He had made a commitment to another woman, and in their tradition he was as good as married.

*****

Mitsui noticed how distracted he was but so was she. They were not a family big on confiding in each other or airing their feelings to each other. She had noticed that he did not talk much at the dinner table, but that was nothing strange. Apart from some business discussion between father and son, nothing much was said, and she was usually left out of the conversation. She picked at her food even though it was one of her favorites: Kushiyaki (a mixture of meat and vegetables) and white rice. It was Wednesday and her usual date with Charles was tomorrow and she could not wait to see him. They called each other two times a day which she could afford to do because her husband left to go to the office from eight and did not come back until around nine. Did he realize how lonely she was? And if he did, would it matter to him? Charles had showed her a glimpse of a better life and she was craving it!

"I think we should maybe have the arrangement in December," John Kamato said suddenly. He had finished eating and pushed his plate away getting ready to leave the dinner table. Both his wife and son looked up at him startled.

"What arrangement?" Peter asked even though he knew what it was.

"The marriage," he clarified. "I don't think we should wait for a year to make it happen. The sooner it is done, the sooner you get control of the company."

Before now, Peter would have felt his heart thundering with excitement, but right now he felt as if he had been sentenced to the death penalty. "I think we should wait for the year," he said casually, not daring to show how repugnant the idea was to him.

"I agree," his mother said swiftly, not looking at her son. "I think we should wait."

John looked at both of them for a minute and then with a shrug of his slim shoulders, he nodded and went from the room.

"Thank you, Mother," Peter told her and before she could say anything he pushed his chair back and left the table. What a family, she thought sadly.

*****

She called him the next day. He was sitting in his office trying to use work to get his mind off his troubles when she called him.

"Are you okay?"

"I am getting there," he said stiffly. He had to keep her at arm's length and he was trying to find a way to never see her again, but so far he had not come up with anything.

"Peter, I am not very experienced, but this much I know. We are attracted to each other and the inevitable is going to happen sooner or later." She paused. "I want it to happen, but it seems to me that you are struggling with something. I appreciate that you do not want to let me in just now, but I am here when you are ready."

"I can't," he told her abruptly.

"Can't do what?" she asked him, puzzled. "Are you married?"

"No," he told her swiftly.

"Good, because that is not a road I intend to travel down. I don't mess with married men. So now that we have that out of the way, why don't we have dinner at a public place this time?" she suggested.

He wanted to say no, but he had to see her even if it was one more time.

"I promise not to touch you," she teased him.

"Are you sure?" he said softly. He could not help the smile curving his lips.

"I am sure. If you touch me first all bets are off," she warned.

"I will try my best not to," he said with a laugh.

"Okay then, we are set."

*****

He was called into his father's office shortly after. John Masato was sitting around his plain desk, reading through a document in his hands.

"Sit." He gestured towards one of the chairs. He had never treated his son more than an employee and as much as Peter resented it he realized that it had made him work harder to prove himself. "Before I married your mother, I had a woman I was attracted to but knew that I would never ask her to marry me because my wife had been chosen for me. I made her aware of the situation and she was contented to be the woman on the side and I took care of her. We saw each other for several months until we got bored with the arrangement and we ended it. You are probably in the same shoes I was in, and I am going to give you a piece of advice. Don't mistake lust for love and remember what you have to lose; a billion dollar company is a powerful incentive." He nodded and indicated that he was finished, not giving the slightest thought that his son had anything to say!

Chapter 4

He felt like the lowest form of a human being. He performed his duty by having dinner at home with his intended bride and suffered through, forcing himself to make conversation while his mind was on Kimberly and when he was going to see her again. He had told himself that dinner with her a week ago would be the last and then he would tell her goodbye, but it had not worked out that way.

He had picked her up from the store and she had wrapped her arms around his neck and put her mouth on his. With a groan, he had placed his arms around her small waist and deepened the kiss, right there in plain view, his body tightening with desire. "I lied," she had told him huskily. He could feel her breasts pressing against his chest and he could not quite filter his thoughts.

"About what?" he had whispered hoarsely.

"Not touching you." She nipped at his bottom lip with his teeth and he felt the shudder went straight through his body! This was not happening; he thought in despair, how could he feel so much for her in such a short time? He bore her back against the vehicle and took her mouth with his helplessly, his hands roaming her body feverishly. It was the glare from the headlights of an oncoming vehicle that brought him back to where they were; standing outside her store for anyone to see them. He had stepped away from her, his hands trembling badly and allowed her to go inside the vehicle.

He did not say anything to her the entire time they were going to the restaurant and she had leaned back her head against the head rest and closed her eyes. He kept looking at her as he drove. He wanted her so much that he did not know how he was going to contain himself around her.

She made him laugh in spite of himself, with some witty repartee about some of her clients and told him about her two best friends, Deidre and Simone, and how they had been friends from college. They were eating at a small unpretentious restaurant just outside of town, and at that time of the evening it was fairly empty. He loved the way the green sweater she was wearing looked against her smooth skin and her totally confident and unabashed laughter. He could not help but compare her to his intended bride and wished she was the one he was going to marry.

"Tell me about them," he said, forcing a smile to his mouth.

"Deidre is full of drama and fancies herself in love with the guy she is dating." She shook her head. "He does not mean her any good and is constantly loafing on her. Simone met someone in Tuscany and she thinks he might be the one."

"How about you?" He picked at the roast beef in his plate. "Ever been in love?"

"No." She looked at him for a moment. "Never been close until now."

His hands became still and he looked at her, his breathing getting shallow.

"Don't worry, I am not going to demand that you marry me or anything like that." She leaned forward. "I like you a lot, Peter Kamato, and I am very attracted to you, but I have no hang ups about anything else."

"I feel the same way." His voice sounded strangled to his ears.

"Good," she exclaimed softly. "Now let's eat."

*****

The dimensions were all wrong. He stared at the specs for a little while longer. It was the supermarket they had acquired recently and were trying to remodel it and get it off the ground for Christmas. The renovations were taking a little bit longer than expected and he was getting impatient with it. Apart from his other duties, he was responsible for acquisitions and he knew his father watched everything he did like a hawk.

He pressed his buzzer. "Jennifer, please get the contractor on the phone."

"Right away, Peter."

*****

"Here you go, Cassie, that's a good girl," Kimberly said soothingly, raising the bottle to the dog's mouth for her to drink down the medicine. She had not been eating too well for the past few days and she had taken her to the vet only to discover that she had colic. "That's a good girl," she said soothingly as the dog finished drinking and went back to lie down, resting her head on her paws and looking at her with sorrowful dark brown eyes.

"Does she look sicker to you?" she asked Brian anxiously. He was cleaning out some poop from the empty cages. It was a little after four, and some of the owners had already collected their pets.

"I am knee deep in crap, so I am not able to answer that," he said, complaining as he went to get rid of the stuff.

"It's part of the job, buddy. I did it all of last week so now this week is yours." She glanced back at Cassie. "I am going to see if she will eat something."

*****

"This is nice," Mitsui said with a soft smile as she snuggled closer to Charles and closed her eyes. It was Thursday and they had met as usual and he had cooked her dinner, some pasta and ground beef, and they had practiced the dance routine they had learned earlier in the week. She had rested her head against his broad shoulder and felt as if everything was going to turn out okay.

He lifted her head and looked down at her. "I want to kiss you properly."

"I have been waiting for that," she told him her heart racing.

He took her lips with his gently, his movements unhurried and she felt as if he had opened up a slow gentle flowing stream inside her. For years, she had been subdued and constrained and not allowed to show her feelings. Sex with her husband the few times they had been together had been mechanical and lifeless, a duty performed because she had to and she had endured it like a dutiful wife. Now with Charles she felt as if she had come home and this was where she belonged. She opened her mouth underneath his and moved against him wanting to feel his wonderful body next to hers.

He lifted her up and carried her slight frame to the bedroom, closing the door behind them before laying her on the bed, looking down at her before joining her.

*****

"Cassie died," she told him mechanically. He had called to find out how she was and she had told him.

"Hey, I am sorry. Do you want me to come over?" he asked her instantly, and she almost told him yes, wanting to feel his arms around her.

"I have to go to my mom's for dinner," she said with a sigh. "Oh Peter, I knew she was ill but I kept hoping she was getting better and I wondered if I had taken her home like my mother said I should she would still be alive."

"Stop blaming yourself, you did the best you could."

"Thanks. See you tomorrow?" she asked him.

"Try and keep me away," he said softly.

*****

"Mom, I cannot eat a single thing else," she protested, refusing the second helping of fried chicken and potato salad her mother was heaping onto her plate.

"Eat, you look too thin," she insisted, going back to sit at her end of the table. "I know you are mourning but you also need to eat."

"I miss her so much," she said with a sigh, automatically picking up a drumstick and taking a bite.

"I know," Karen said sympathetically. "Now tell me about this young man you have been seeing and why have I not been introduced to him."

"How did you know?" Kimberly looked at her startled.

"I am not some old and doddering woman who does not notice what goes on around her," her mother said mildly. "You look different and you hardly have time to call or come and see your mother. Now that usually means that a man is in the picture."

"It's a thing," she said reluctantly. She put down the half-eaten drumstick and looked at her mother. "He is struggling with something and I am waiting for him to tell me what it is."

"How do you feel about him?" Her mother got up to get them some orange juice.

"I like him a lot and I haven't felt this way about anyone else." She shrugged eloquently. "I am just seeing where it is leading."

"What about him?"

"I think he feels the same way."

*****

He knew they were going to make love and he had shed all of the thoughts flooding his mind about why he should stay away from her. She needed him, he argued with himself, she was grieving her pet and she needed him and there was no way he was going to stay away when she needed comfort. It was Friday night, the day after Thanksgiving, and she had spent the day with her mother and felt a little better when she went home.

He arrived on her doorstep promptly at eight with a bottle of wine and a stuffed dog that looked a lot like Cassie. She wanted to cry right then and there at his thoughtfulness. Instead, she put her arms around his neck and dragged his head down for a kiss that shook both of them to the core. "Kimberly." He gathered her up in his arms and carried her to the couch, only stopping long enough to put the things he had brought on the table.

"I want to feel you," she murmured, pulling his corded sweater over his head, followed by his white t-shirt. His chest was smooth and muscled and his waist narrow. "I don't care about anything else, I just want to feel you."

With a groan, he took her lips with his, deepening the kiss and digging his fingers into her thick hair. He stopped kissing her and pulled her sweatshirt over her head, his eyes narrowed as he looked at her unfettered breasts. He bent his head and took a nipple inside his mouth pulling on it hungrily. Kimberly arched her back against him feeling the pull straight to the core of her. He moved to the other nipple sucking it into his mouth, his tongue flicking over it and fanning the fire inside her.

He lifted his head to look at her. "Are you sure?" he asked her thickly, his eyes on her passion filled face.

"If you stop now, I am going to kill you," she told him huskily. She took one of his hands and placed it over her breast. "I am on fire for you."

He picked her up and took her into the tiny bedroom where he placed her on the bed and finished undressing her. She watched him as he bent down on the side of the bed and pulled off her panties. His fingers parted the lips of her vagina and he ran a finger between them watching her reaction. She squirmed and arched her body as his finger touched her mound before dipping it inside her again. She opened her legs to him and he thrust his fingers inside her over and over again. He wanted to please her and let her know what was coming. "I can't stay away from you, please help me." It was said like a prayer and she had a feeling he was talking to himself. He pulled out and finished undressing and stood before her. She stared at him shocked and surprised as she noticed his erection. She knew she had to tell him now.

"I have never been with a man like that," she whispered.

"I suspected," he told her gently as he crouched before her. "I will try not to hurt you." His body felt as if it was exploding! He wanted to explore every inch of her body. He did not care what happened after this, but he just wanted to feel her and be with her. He entered her a little bit at a time and felt her close around him tightly. He stopped and framed her face with his hands, a wry smile on his face. "I have never met anyone like you." He pushed into her and tried to distract her with his words. "I am not used to someone like you and I find myself being surprised every time I talk to you or I am with you." He pushed inside her without warning and she cried out sharply as he cleared the barrier, her body arched against his, arms clinging to him. He swallowed her cries inside his mouth. He waited for her to adjust to his erection and then he started moving inside her, slowly at first then increasing the pace as she moved with him. Kimberly dug her fingers into his shoulders and wrapped her legs around his waist, lifting her hips as the fire inside her refused to be quenched!

He felt the pressure building up and he knew he did not want it to end just now. He wanted to go on for the entire night and he did not want to be with anyone else but her. His thrust became desperate and he held her closer to him, his mouth soft on hers, their bodies moving together so in sync that they were almost as one, their souls touching and mingling, flying high on the desire that coursed through them.

They came together in a crescendo of music and she clung to him, the unfamiliar emotion lifting her body against his. He held her closer to him and called out her name, his body shuddering against hers. They were both swept away by the strange new feeling and the almost overwhelming wave that carried them along!

He kissed her eyes, her cheeks and her nose and then her mouth, his tongue venturing in and exploring. Kimberly was still trying to recover from the maelstrom still rocking her body with its force.

They held each other and she curled up against him and drifted off to sleep. He held her and stared off into the darkened room. He had thought it was just an attraction and maybe he could have her and then after he got married he would be able to look at it as a wonderful experience and remember it when he was in his loveless marriage. But it had become more than that, so much more. His body was hers and tonight had proven that. How could he go back from this? How was he go into a loveless marriage after this intense emotion he shared with her? How could he stay away from her knowing that she held the most important part of him inside her? What the hell was he going to do?

She woke up and stirred against him, stretching languidly, her breath on his chest. "I want you to stay, please?" she murmured.

"I can't leave," he told her hoarsely. He bent his head and kissed her desperately, reaching between them and inserting his erection inside her.

She sighed and closed her arms around him, closing her eyes as he moved inside her again!

*****

He did not leave until late that afternoon because they had not left the bed until way past noon. He had woke her up with his mouth on her body exploring every inch of it and she had felt the passion unleashed inside her as his mouth wandered over her body.

"Want to go out for breakfast?" he asked her gently. They had showered together and it had further delayed them. "Or lunch?"

"Hmm." She wrapped her hands around his neck and standing on her toes she kissed him softly. "I guess," she murmured. She stepped out of his arms and started dressing. She pulled on black leggings and a red sweater and knee-length boots. She twisted her thick hair into a bun and applied lipstick and eye shadow and she was ready.

They went to a pancake place out of town and had stacks of pancakes with whipped cream and coffee. "I don't I can move," she said rubbing her hand over her tummy. "You should have stopped me, Peter."

"I enjoyed seeing you gorge," he told her in amusement. She had whipped cream on the side of her lips and he used his thumb to wipe it away.

They were so engrossed in each other that they did not notice someone watching them and then hurried away.

*****

"I thought you wanted to try this place," Charles looked at her puzzled as she hurried back inside the car.

"Please drive," she told him quietly, visibly shaken. John had gone to a meeting for the day and she had decided to take the chance to be with the man she was starting to fall in love with. And he had decided to take her to a little pancake place he knew that served this side of town. She knew her son had not come home last night and her husband had not said anything to her, but he never usually did.

"Are you going to tell me what's going on?" he asked her as soon as they reached a little distance.

"We are kidding ourselves by being together like this." She was near tears as she felt her world crumbling around her. She was having an affair and cheating on her husband and it does not matter that she kept telling herself that she was trapped in a loveless marriage, the fact remained that she was in a marriage and the commitment meant that she was in it until death. Seeing her son with that girl and the way they looked at each had triggered something inside her. He was basically in the same position as she was. He was not physically married to the girl that had been picked out for him, but they were bound together by a contract that was as strong as the marriage contract itself. Her poor son!

Charles stopped the car and turned to face her. "What happened back there?" He was ready to ask her to leave her husband and marry him, he knew it was not going to be easy to do but he would wait because he had fallen in love with her and he never expected to be getting a second chance at love. If she was in love with her husband, he would have walked away even though he felt this way.

"We have to be hiding, at least I have to be hiding because I happen to be married and I am bound to someone else." She was not about to tell him about what she had seen at the pancake place.

"I know we did not sign up for this, Mits, it just happened and we could not help it." He turned her to face him. "I am not losing you," he told her gently but firmly.

She stared at him and bursting into tears, she went inside his arms.

*****

He finally went home in the late afternoon. He had wanted to stay so much, but he knew staying one more night was going to lead him to want to stay another and another. Neither of his parents were there and he was happy about that because he wanted to be alone with his thoughts. He went straight up to his suite of rooms and stood at the window looking over the already darkened grounds. It was almost December, and he was not looking forward to it because he knew he wanted to spend it with her. He shuddered as he remembered her body underneath his! The explosion of desire and the way he had swelled inside her and the way she had closed around him like a well-fitting glove. His heart shuddered a little bit as he wondered if she was pregnant. It was something he had considered and thought about using protection, but he had swept the thought away. What if that happened? Would his father forgive him enough to allow him to marry her and hand the company over to him? Now he was not so sure the company meant anything to him anymore. He knew she meant more to him than anything else and he did not want to lose her!

*****

Kimberly stripped and pulled on her nightgown as she got ready to go to bed. She had never felt such an onslaught of emotions in her life and she knew her body was not going to feel the same way again!

Chapter 5

There was a discreet knock on the door of his bedroom and he frowned wondering who it could be. His father had gone on an overnight trip out of town and he had not seen his mother when he came in. The night air was chilly and they had thought it would have snowed for Christmas, but they only gotten a few flurries. He had spent the evening with Kimberly and had driven home reluctantly. "Come in," he called out briefly.

His mother came inside slowly and he looked at her in surprise. "Mother, are you okay?" he asked her formally.

She nodded and stood by the door her hands folded.

"Please sit," he said politely, indicating one of the several sofas in the room. He had changed and showered and had pulled on a sweatpants and a t-shirt.

"I have not been inside your rooms since you were a teenager," she smiled slightly, perching on the edge of the chair and looking around at the purely masculine and impersonal room. "You have not done much with it except removed the posters."

"What is it, Mother?"

"I know you are unhappy with the arrangement your father has made for you." She folded her hands inside her lap and stared down at them. "I never have a say about what happens in this house or in the business. I am regarded as a very decorative addition and I have come to live with it because it's our tradition. I sense that you want more and you are struggling with it, maybe you have met someone and realized that what we believe is not all there is to life."

Peter looked at her in surprise. For the entire time he had known his mother, she had never hugged him or told him that she loved him and had hardly spoken to him but had left everything to his father who ran the home like he ran his business, with an iron hand and he would never dreamed of going to her to confide and ask for advice. "You seem okay with the arrangement," he said to her briefly.

"I have never known any other arrangement," she said, looking at him closely. He looked more like her than he did his father, only taking his height. He was extremely handsome but very somber and looked unapproachable, except when she had seen him with that girl at the pancake place. "But there is still hope for you," she told him.

"You make it sound like a death sentence." His mouth twisted into a facsimile of a smile and he moved over to look out the window, noticing absently the wind blowing the bare twigs on the trees, giving them a ghostly appearance.

"Sometimes it feels that way," she told him frankly.

"And yet you stayed," he commented, turning to look at her.

"I stayed because I have parents who would disown me if I ever left and I stayed because I had a son to think about."

He came over and sat on the seat opposite hers. He had never known she felt the way she did and he suddenly felt his heart going out to her. His father was not an easy man to live with and never shown the slightest hint of emotion and he provided for them but that was it. "You stayed because of me?"

"That was the biggest part of it," she said with a smile. "I am duty bound to stay with him, Peter, but you have not taken the vows yet so there is still time for you."

"Mother, what are you saying?" His eyes narrowed as he stared at her.

"I know the company means a lot to you because you have worked so hard since you were a little boy and he promised to hand the reign over to you, but there comes a time when you have to decide if it's worth giving up something worthwhile for."

"What do you think you know, Mother?" He was not willing to tell her about Kimberly, he was not comfortable with her that way. She was his mother and she was a stranger.

"I know your heart is not in it," she told him sadly. "I don't want you to end up like us in a loveless marriage because of tradition."

"But you have money to spend any way you want to and you do not lack anything materially. You live in a big house with people at you beck and call and credit cards with unlimited money on them. Isn't that worth it?" He had leaned forward in his seat and looked at her closely.

"What do you think?" She looked him squarely in the face.

"I think you would give it all up for love and happiness," he said slowly. "So would I," he said quietly.

*****

"I think he looks okay now, Marlene," Kimberly said, looking at the little furry dog closely. He had been looking listless and not his usual vibrant self the other day, but she could see that he was coming around.

"I think he misses me a lot when I am away," the woman said worriedly. "Don't you, my baby?" She took her pet from Kimberly and kissed his wet nose fondly. "Thanks," she told the girl with a smile before heading out.

"I think that woman needs to get herself a man," Brian murmured as soon as the thin-looking woman exited the store.

"Keep your voice down!" Kimberly rebuked him mildly, trying not to encourage him. It was three in the afternoon and December was coming to a close with snow and rain intermittently. He was giving the cats their last meal for the day before the owners came to get them. He had told her that his girlfriend had left him the week before Christmas and he had been down ever since. Her mother had invited him over for dinner several evenings and he had been so grateful, he had cleared away the snow for her. "Maybe you can put that in your application now that you are single again," she told him teasingly.

"Not my type," he muttered, giving her a pained look before going off to empty and clean the bowls.

*****

He picked her up from the store that evening and loaded her bike into the back of his vehicle. Brian had left earlier, claiming that he was going to cook himself something and enjoy his single life with a glass of wine and some sports.

They picked up some Italian food on the way and he took the packages from her and went inside the house while she secured her bike in the store room.

"How about hot chocolate to warm us up first?" she suggested. She noticed that he was silent more than usual and he seemed preoccupied.

"Can we talk a little bit first?" he asked her quietly, leading the way to the sofa and taking off his suit jacket and spreading it over the back of the sofa. She sat opposite him, suspecting that he had something very important to say to her.

"What is it, Peter?"

"Have you heard about Kamato Holdings?"

She frowned and shook her head no. "Should I have?"

He mentioned the name of a supermarket and the department store she shopped sometimes. "We acquire defunct businesses and fix them up and put our people in them. Sometimes we allow the staff already there to stay."

"You said we." She looked at him curiously and put two and two together. "You are Kamato Holdings and you own supermarkets and stores all over the country?" She looked at him in shock. She had never put it together because she had never felt it mattered. She had thought he was in corporate and suspected he had money, but she also thought it was just a very well-placed position in a company, not this!

"My father built the company, expanding it from a supermarket his father owned when he brought them over from Japan. When he inherited it, he expanded, and now it is a billion dollar company." He paused, his eyes on hers. "I am supposed to take over from him, but there is a condition attached: I have to marry a Japanese girl who has already been picked out for me."

She sat there staring at him for so long that he wondered if he had lost her, wondered if he should have told her. He could have gone on as if everything was okay, but he was thinking that time was running out and he still did not know what to do.

"Say something," he said urgently.

"You should have told me," she said slowly, feeling as if her world was crashing down on her. She had never asked him about permanency, but she had taken it for granted that they would get there eventually.

"When?" He stood up when she did and watched as she moved away from him. "I met you when you almost injured me with your bike," he said, smiling grimly. "I never expected to feel this way about you, Kimberly. I thought it was just something we would get out of our system, I never expected this." His voice was pleading.

"I know." She surprised him by answering that way. "I never thought this would evolve into something so intense, it took me by surprise. Have you met her?"

"Yes," he said with a sad smile. "We had several chaperoned dinners at the house with her parents and mine." He came over towards her and took her hands in his. "I was okay to marry her and take over from my father because I worked hard to reach there, but now I don't think I can."

She pulled her hands away from him and stared up at him. "What do you mean?"

"I mean that feeling the way I do about you I cannot marry someone else," he told her frankly.

"You think I would allow you to give up a billion dollar company in order to be with me?" she asked him, her eyebrows raised.

"You would not be the one allowing me, Kimberly," he said, his voice tight. "I cannot be with someone else and I really hope you are not implying that you are contented to be my mistress."

"I am not the mistress type," she told him loftily, rubbing her hands over her arms to ward off the sudden chill.

"I know that and I don't want you to be my mistress." He came and stood in front of her. "Tell me to leave you alone and I will try and do so as hard as it will be. I don't want to hurt you, Kimberly."

"I cannot tell you to leave me alone." She went on her toes and framed his face, taking in the misery and the lost look in his expression. "I have never felt this way before and as long as we can be together then we will be. I am not going to tell you to leave the company that is rightfully yours so you can be with me, I cannot take that responsibility, but in the meantime I want to be with you."

His body shuddered in relief and he lifted her into his arms and they went to the bedroom. "Thank you," he told her hoarsely, pulling off the denim she had on and throwing it on the floor followed by the thick blue sweater she had on. He stood there looking at her in a black sheer bra and panties and he felt himself harden even more. He could never give her up for anything, but he did not want to think about it right now.

He took off his clothes and joined her on the bed. "I want you so badly that I cannot keep still."

"I want you to take me where I love to go," she whispered and pulled down his head and he crushed her lips with his, pulling her underneath him and covering her body with his!

*****

He told her about growing up with parents who had never hugged him or interacted with him in any way. "I thought it was a way of life until I went to college and I met some of my roommate's parents and saw the love there and the relationship they had and never realized that I was craving more." He rested his head on her forehead, his semi-erect penis inside her. "I want a life with you, Kimberly," he whispered, taking her lips with his again, his touch gentle.

"So do I." She arched her body against his, and with a groan he moved inside her, his breath shuddering inside his chest.

*****

"So, when are we going to meet this mystery man of yours?" Simone asked her. They were at Deidre's apartment where they were spending New Year's Day together. The guy she had met in Tuscany, Lorenzo, had come over for the Christmas holiday and they had spent the entire time together, but he had to go back yesterday because something had come up with the farm. So both friends had decided to keep her company for the holiday. Kimberly's mother had gone to a concert.

Kimberly hesitated. She had thought about what she should tell her friends and her mother. After that night when he had told her about his predicament, he had spent the night with her and they had talked way into the night, but they had stayed away from trying to find a solution. The fact remained that they were in a forbidden relationship, and although she knew she could not give him up now, she was not going to dwell on it.

"There is something I need to tell you." She took her wine and wandered over to the sofa closest to the fireplace. Her friend's apartment was in one of those ultra modern buildings that always looked pristine and very clean and shiny. She had inherited money from her aunt who had died a year ago and had decided to invest into the apartment.

"I told you he is Japanese, right?" she asked them. They nodded and looked at her curiously. "Ever heard about Kamato Holdings?"

"Of course," Deidre said immediately. "We have done business with them in the past. They own supermarkets and stores all over the country and even a hotel downtown. Why?"

"His name is Peter Kamato," she told them wryly.

"You are dating a billionaire?" Simone looked at her in shock.

"It' a little more complicated than that." Kimberly put aside her wine glass and sat back in the deep seated sofa. She told them the Japanese tradition and how he was supposed to marry a Japanese girl who was already picked out for him.

Her friends stared at her in amazement. "What are you going to do?" Simone asked her quietly.

"For now? Nothing." She smiled slightly. "I have never felt this way about a man before and I am not willing to just let him go like that and he feels the same way. However, I am not going to stand in the way of him getting the company that rightfully belongs to him." She looked down at her clasped hands. "We have several months before he has to make good on his promise, so we will be spending as much time as possible together."

"Honey." Deidre came over and sat on the arm of the sofa. "It sounds so romantic and it also sounds as if you love him and he feels the same. I am romantic enough to believe that it is going to work out."

"I am not going to be thinking that far," Kimberly admitted. "But I cannot help but think about the girl who was chosen for him. What if she is in love with him and do I have any right to be standing in her way?"

"I strongly doubt that," Simone said dryly. "These matches are not designed for love. It is either there is something mutually beneficial to the parties involved or the parents want to control the person the son or daughter marries. I am sure it's the latter because Kamato Holdings is a billion dollar company and does not need anything else to make it viable."

"I am definitely not going to be on the favored list," Kimberly said ironically. "I am a black woman with no money, so I am definitely not suitable."

"We do not choose who we love," Deidre said with a wistful smile. "We cannot help how we feel towards another person, and as long as it is set in motion, there is no way we can stop it."

*****

"I spoke to him for the first time, Charles, and we actually had a conversation." Mitsui's face was lit with a smile. They were spending the day cuddled up to each other in front of the fire. He had ordered take-out and they had eaten and then relaxed. Her husband had gone for the day and night and she remembered feeling so happy that he was out of the house. Peter had not come home the night before and she suspected he was spending time with her. She looked like such a beautiful vibrant girl, and she could see why her son would be attracted to her.

"And what is the relationship between you now?" Charles asked her gently. He had encouraged her to change the way she dealt with her son and be the one to reach out.

"He is not one for conversations, but when he comes down in the mornings, he would ask me how I am doing and he never usually asked that," she responded.

"So, it is improving?" he commented, hugging her to him. He had fallen in love with her and did not know what was going to happen, but he knew he was happy for the first time since he had lost his beloved wife.

"I would like to think so." She rested her head against his chest. "I am going to keep trying."

*****

"We are going out," she called him the next day. She had closed the store on New Year's Day and they had opened back up today with the snow pelting down and covering everything in sight. She had ridden her bike in spite of it and had rushed inside the store almost freezing to death. They had not had a lot of customers today because of the weather and she was considering closing early.

"Where are we going?" he asked her indulgently. They had gotten closer since he had confessed to her and now she found she wanted to spend as much time with him as possible.

"How about going away for the night at this little inn in the country that I hear serves the best lamb chops?" she suggested.

"I would love that," he said softly. "I will pick you up shortly. I just have to get some things done and then I will be right there."

*****

John Kamato rolled out of bed and shoved his hands through his dark hair streaked with grey. He had told his wife that he was going on a business trip, but he had lied, not that he owed her any explanation anyway. He looked up as the girl strolled out of the bathroom, completely naked. She was blonde and blue eyed and he had been seeing her for the past two months and he could not get enough of her. She made him feel like dynamite in bed, not like his icicle of a wife. She was a little on the young side, being only twenty-six and a little empty headed, but she more than satisfied in the bedroom. He had set her up in an apartment and paid all her bills and tried to get away to be with her whenever he could. He did not feel any sense of guilt whatsoever because it was not like he was in love with his wife and he did not owe her any loyalty.

"Hi daddy," Stephanie said with a giggle as she waltzed over to him, her large breasts bouncing. "What do you want me to do for you now?"

"You know what I want," he growled, pulling her down on his lap. She always excited him and he had met her as he was looking at a building they had acquired. She was working in one of the supermarkets he owned and recently she told him she wanted to quit the job and stay at home. But he did not believe in taking care of someone who stayed at home all day, no matter how much they excite him!

Chapter 6

Their love bloomed! It was as if the forbidden aspect of it intensified it more. They spent every available time together and they made love whenever they got the chance. He kept hoping that she would get pregnant and his father would be forced to realize that the arrangement between him and Natsuko would be null and void, but he admitted reluctantly to himself that he did not want a child with her that way. He took her out to places and spent every special moment together. He insisted on giving her gifts, expensive gifts that she argued with him about.

"I don't need gifts, Peter," she told him firmly when he brought an exquisite pair of diamond earrings for her on Valentine's Day weekend. They had planned to spend the time at home because she had told him she did not want to spend the time with other people around but just with him. They were aware that the time was coming when he would have to make a decision that would affect them drastically.

"I don't see anything wrong with giving the woman I love gifts," he told her firmly. She went still and looked up at him. He was busy unscrewing the wine to pour the liquid into the glasses.

They had not told each other of their love, but it was always implied.

"I love you too," she told him softly. He looked up at her, his dark eyes speaking volumes.

"I know," he said thickly, moving towards her.

"Stop!" She put out her hands to halt his progress towards her. "You are not the only bearing gifts. She pulled off the loose black cotton dress she had on and he felt himself hardening fiercely when he looked at what she was wearing. It was red! An all-in-one teddy with deep plunging neckline that stopped just above her navel and the legs were cut high above her thighs showing glimpses of the curl of hair on her pubic area. Her nipples were large and transparent through the sheer material. "Take off your clothes," she ordered huskily. He felt himself shudder as he undressed. The women he had been with before had always been content for him to take charge and he had done so because he was used to it, but with her it was different, she was confident and lack guile and was not hung up on him being in charge all the time.

He stepped out of his underwear and held his throbbing penis in one hand, looking at her. He was bursting! She had on black heels and walked towards the table to pour a glass of wine taking it over to him for him to take a sip, which he did and she took one after. She did not swallow all of hers but went down on her knees before him.

"What are you doing?" he asked her in a strangled voice.

"Shh," she whispered, taking his penis in her hands. The liquid was still in her mouth and when she closed her mouth over him, the sensation of the cold liquid against his skin almost drove him crazy! She pulled him inside her mouth swirling the wine around his penis sucking on the tip of it. He felt his control crumbling like a tower of dominoes crashing to the floor. She was not finished with him yet. She cupped his testicles in one hand and squeezed gently, spiraling him almost over the edge. He was not going to last long he knew that, his body shuddering as he felt the sensation washing over him.

"I can't hold back," he told her tightly, and with a hoarse cry, he joined her on the floor and entered her immediately. He clung to her and took her lips with his hungrily, his thrusts urgent and demanding. He knew he could not wait on her and with a cry that sounded tortured he emptied himself inside her!

She came soon after and he was still spilling his seed inside her as he would never stop, his body shuddering on top of hers!

*****

"What if you are pregnant?" he asked her quietly as they lay in bed after with her resting her head on his chest. They had finished the bottle of wine and ate the éclairs he had brought as well.

She lifted her head and looked down at him. "That's not the answer, Peter, and we both know it."

"I am not letting you go, Kimberly," he warned her, his intense dark eyes holding hers. "I don't want to live without you."

"Do you think I want to be without you?" she asked him softly, combing the soft dark hair off his forehead. "I shudder to think about it, so I don't, but getting pregnant as a way out is not the solution. I just have to believe that it will work out somehow."

"I am supposed to have dinner with her and her parents on Sunday," he murmured and felt her stiffened slightly against him. "If you tell me it is hurting you for me to do so, I will find a way to skip it." He held the back of her neck and forced her to look at him.

"How can I, Peter?" she asked him sadly. "How am I going to tell you to ignore your family's tradition because of some unreasonable jealousy I am feeling?"

"You have no need to feel jealous, baby," he insisted. "I am yours only and you know that."

"I know." She climbed on top of him. "I need to be reassured."

He did so quite effectively.

*****

Kimberly told her mother about him. She had invited her over for Sunday dinner and she had accepted, knowing that if she stayed home she would be thinking of him having dinner with her and her parents and it would drive her crazy.

He had called her during the day and had told her he would come over later and asked her please not to think about it too much. She had told him she would go over to her mother's for dinner.

The end of February was drawing near and the weather was still bleak and unpredictable. Snow had fallen the night before and gave the place a beautiful white glare that looked dazzling to the eyes. Her mother's place was situated way back from the road that gave it a seclusion and privacy that made it like a serene and secure haven. The trees that lined the driveway were covered in snow and the swing in the front yard moved back and forth eerily. Kimberly remembered days on the swing when she came home from school and how she would dream that she had a brother or a sister to play with, until with a determination that had served her well throughout life she had started to entertain herself by teaching herself games that boys usually played. Her father had built a tree house for her and she had spent a lot of her time there just camping out.

"How are you, dear?" Karen asked her as she placed a bowl of fresh fruits in front of her. They were in her cozy kitchen with the smell of pot roast beef simmering on the stovetop and an apple pie cooling on the rack.

"I am okay," Kimberly said with a smile, popping one of the grapes inside her mouth. "I was thinking about dad and how much I miss him."

"I miss him too." Her mother poured two cups of tea and slid one over to her before taking a seat beside her. "Everything all right?"

"I met someone," Kimberly closed her hands around the warmth of the cup and stared down into the dark brown liquid. "We have been seeing each other for the past six months."

"And yet I have not met him," her mother murmured.

"It's complicated," Kimberly said with a little laugh. She told her mother about him and about the situation. "Sometimes I feel like we are cheating on that poor girl. I convinced myself at one point that I have to end it, Mom, but I can't find the strength to do so. He said he is willing to give up the company but he is not willing to give me up. How can I ask him to do that?"

"I have a feeling he is not asking you to do that, dear." Karen looked at her only child searchingly. She had watched her grow up strong and very opinionated and watched her blossom into a beautiful young woman who knew what she wanted and did not settle for anything else and she was so proud of her. "It's not a love match as you said and as he told you too and I cannot imagine marrying someone I am not in love with, but then again I am not used to that. He met you and it changed things for him, so can you even imagine how confusing it must be for him?"

"When I am with him, I feel like I have it all. I don't care about his money and I never asked him about it, all I want is him but I cannot tell him to come and live with me and let us get married and we will work it out." She sighed and stared down at her rapidly cooling tea. "We have such a short time left together and I am so scared of losing him."

"It will work out." Karen reached out and squeezed her daughter's hands lightly. "In the meantime, I would like to meet him."

*****

He had reservations about meeting her mother because he could not take her to meet his parents. "I know why you are not able to, Peter," she had told him quietly. "I have told my mom about the situation and she wants to meet you."

"Are you sure she does not hate me?" he asked her soberly. He had come over like he promised and she had launched herself into his arms as soon as he opened the door. He had held her to him tightly, lifting her petite frame and taking her over to the sofa where he cradled her in his arms.

"I have told her how wonderful you are, so how could she?" she asked him saucily. She had seen the haunted expression on his face and knew that the dinner had been hard on him.

"You did?" he rested his head against hers and sighed, closing his eyes. All through dinner he had been thinking of her and could not wait for it to end so that he could come over to be with her. He had been forced to sit in the living room and try and have a conversation with Natsuko. The poor girl had kept her eyes downcast for the entire time and had answered his questions in monosyllables. He had a glimpse of what marrying her would be like and he would prefer death over it. With a sudden movement, he pushed up her t-shirt and cupped her unfettered breasts in his palms, his thumbs passing over the nipples. She arched her back and when he bent his dark head to take a nipple inside his mouth she dissolved. He sucked the nipple inside his mouth urgently, one hand reaching underneath her t-shirt to move the edge of her panties to seek her wetness. He worked two fingers inside her rapidly, and Kimberly clamped her thighs closed and moved against his thrusts. He eased her off his lap and onto the couch, kneeling over her, his mouth still on her nipple. She opened her legs wide as he increased the thrusts of his fingers inside her. He left her nipple and ventured down, his mouth going on her mound, his fingers still working inside her, his teeth grazing her. He removed his fingers and it was replaced by his tongue as his hands held her legs aloft as he brought her to the peak of pleasure, his tongue moving inside her, tasting the passion and desire that flooded his mouth!

*****

They had dinner with her mother on Monday evening, and she took an instant liking to him. He was so quaintly formal and although a little aloof, Karen was fascinated at how different he was and how his face softened whenever he spoke to or looked at her daughter. He was clearly in love with her and it was very obvious.

"This is very good, Karen," he told her politely. He had started referring to her by her first name when she had told him to do so. She had cooked roast beef and potato salad along with sweet corn and raisins.

"Thank you, Peter," she said with a smile. "Have you gotten my daughter to cook for you yet?"

"She told me she did not cook." His eyes met hers and suddenly Karen saw it. When they looked at each other, it was as if there was no one else in the room. The electricity between them was so charged that it was tangible.

"That's right, mister, so don't start getting any ideas that I am going to be slaving over a stove just to get you something warm in your belly when there are so many take out options," she told him darkly.

Her mother watched as he smiled at her gently, his eyes going over her face as he could not get enough of her. She felt humbled and somewhat petrified at the love they shared and hoped it would get a chance to blossom.

*****

"I like him," her mother told her when they were in the kitchen tidying up and Peter was sitting in the living room having dessert. "And he loves you." She looked at her daughter for a minute. "You have the real thing and I want to tell you that somehow it is going to work out for both of you. That man is head over heels in love with you."

"He is not the only one." Her eyes drifted to where he was and a smile creased her lips. "I feel the same way."

*****

"Come in," the deep voice called out briefly. Peter pushed the door to his father's office open and stepped inside. The man sitting behind the massive desk looked up at his only son and continued reading the document before him. "What is it, Peter?"

"We need to talk about the marriage arrangement," Peter told him, coming closer to the desk but remained standing.

His father put aside the document reluctantly and leaned back in his chair, his attention on him. "What about it?"

"I met someone," Peter told him briefly, holding his gaze.

"Ah." The single word was loaded with meaning. "Sit, please." He gestured towards one of the chairs and Peter took a seat reluctantly. "You fancy yourself in love with this woman and believe that she is worth throwing away your company for."

They stared at each other before Peter gave his answer. "I am in love with her and I was hoping you would see things my way and want me to be happy above anything else."

His father gave a short bark of laughter that had no ring of amusement in it at all. "How happy are you going to be when there is no money to maintain the lifestyle you have been accustomed to? And how content will she be when she discovers that you do not have a cent to your name?"

Peter bristled with despair and anger towards a man who was so hard and cold that he would prefer his only child to be trapped into a loveless marriage than to be happy. "Who are you going to leave the company to, Father?" Peter asked him coldly, not in the least bit intimidated by him. "Michael Evans, the CFO, who spends his spare time gambling away his very substantial earnings? Or old Barrington McGregor who has been divorced three times and is drowning in alimonies? Need I go on or do you get the picture?"

"You dare to challenge me?" John Kamato's voice had dropped to a sinister level and he stared at his son unflinchingly.

Peter returned the stare, not backing down. "I was hoping you would not see it as a challenge."

"She might be a good screw," he said scathingly, ignoring the flash of anger in his son's eyes. "Hell, she might even be a great lay! But I really don't see you giving up the company you worked so hard for a piece of tail do you?"

Peter stood up and an incredible calm came over him, replacing the crushing anger he had experienced at his father's words. "You don't know me," he told him coldly. "You never took the time to do so and I refuse to be tied to a woman I do not love, no matter what the benefits."

"We'll see about that!" John Kamato called out furiously as he reached the door.

*****

He ploughed into her viciously causing her to cry out as his fingers dug into her smooth white flesh. He had gone to her straight from work, his blood boiling inside him. How dare he challenge his leadership! She had met him at the door with a drink in hand as was customary and he had downed the whiskey in one gulp and told her harshly to undress. He had taken her right there by the door, entering her forcefully and squeezing her generous breasts cruelly as he thrust inside her.

"Daddy, what's wrong?" she asked him childishly, her lips trembling.

"Shut up," he growled, feeling the disgust crawl inside him and then with a hoarse cry he spilled his seed inside her, his body shuddering.

*****

Peter paced the length of the small living room, his hands clenched at his sides. Kimberly watched him as she sat curled up on the sofa. He had called her and told her he was coming over after work, and he was going to pick her up from the store. He had done so in complete silence, and she had allowed the silence until they reached her place. "What's eating you?" she asked him as she hung up her coat and his and went to sit on the sofa. He did not answer her for a few minutes and she waited on him to do so.

"I asked him about it, I told him I met someone and he will not see reason." He stopped pacing and turned to face her.

"I see." She looked up at him. For a few weeks now, she realized that it had been eating at him and she had tried to take his mind off it. "Did you expect him to?"

"I hoped he would see that I was in love with you and as my father want me to be happy." He crouched before her and held her knees. "I hate this, Kimberly. I want to go out with you and be seen with you as the woman I am totally in love with and I want to marry you and have a family with you."

She closed her hands over his and looked down into his handsome face as if memorizing every feature. The way his dark hair was always falling on his forehead, the cute little dimple in his strong chin, and the mouth that always drove her crazy with need. She never knew she would fall in love like this and she knew she told herself she would be able to give him up when the time came but now she was not so sure about that."I love you so much, Peter, and I hate that you are making yourself crazy over it. I don't know how you feel because I don't have a billion dollar company at stake. It's simple for me because I know I am totally in love with you and marriage or not, that will never change. For now, I just want us to enjoy each other and not think about what is going to happen tomorrow or the next day. I want to concentrate on loving you."

He pulled her down on him and they sat on the carpeted floor. "I wanted to lunge at him and for a moment I forgot he was my father. I saw how much he was enjoying seeing me so torn and I wanted to kill him for not being my father." He tipped her chin up and their eyes met. "But you are right. We need to enjoy each other now and not worry about it until it is right here. I love you, Kimberly, and nothing is going to keep me away from you."

"It better not," she told him huskily as she took his lips with hers.

Chapter 7

"I thought you would be sleeping," her husband's soft sinister voice stirred from her from the sleep she had been drifting into. Mitsui jumped up startled. He never came into her room and he had not touched her in years, but now he was sitting at the edge of the bed still in his shirt and tie he had worn to the office this morning. A glance at the clock told her that it was almost ten o'clock and she wondered where he was coming from, not that she cared.

"What are you doing here, John?" she asked him, pulling the sheets up to her neck. He smelled as if he had been drinking.

"Your son fancies himself in love," he told her caustically, his amused gaze taking in the way she gripped the sheets around her.

"Maybe we should let him choose his own bride," she ventured carefully. In all the years they had been married, she had never gone against his decision until now.

"You too?" His tone was silky soft. "Are you ganging up on me now?"

"It's not about you, John. It's about Peter and what he wants."

"We have been married for a number of years and still are. Do you think if we had been in love we would still be married?"

Mitsui listened to his skewered reasoning and felt the sadness invading her body. She had always knew there was more to marriage than what she shared with him but had not known what it was until she had been with Charles. "We got married because it was forced on us, we never had a say in any of it and because of that we don't talk to each other. This is not a marriage, John, it's an arrangement."

"An arrangement that has worked so far!" he said harshly. "I am not going to allow him to mess up what I have done. If he chooses to marry someone else, he will not be a part of the company and that's final."

"He is your son! Your own flesh and blood. Why can't you find it in your heart to love him and put his interests first? Is it so hard that he has found love?"

He climbed on top of the bed and came closer to her. She cringed and scooted to the head of the bed, her body trembling slightly. "Don't worry," he said looking at her in contempt. "I never felt anything for you before and I certainly do not feel anything now." He got off the bed. "The arrangement stands and if you and your son do not like it you can get the hell out!" With that, he strode out the door, slamming it shut behind him.

Mitsui got off the bed hastily with trembling legs and went and locked the door, sliding down to the floor, her body trembling. How was she going to escape?

*****

Peter did not care anymore. He took Kimberly out with him and did not care who saw them together. He spent most of his nights with her. He did not have a confrontation with his father again, but he knew he was just waiting until the required year deadline before he made his move.

"How about a movie?" Kimberly wrapped her hands around his neck as soon as she had locked the door to store after the last clients had collected their pets. He had come to pick her up as usual and they were in the store together. He was sitting on one of the tables and she was standing between his legs.

"Let's get married," he said suddenly.

"What?" She stared at him, thinking that she had not heard him right.

"We could do it this weekend. We could pick up the rings and go get the license and do a private ceremony." The idea had been germinating inside his head for some time and now it had taken root.

"Do you know what you are saying?" she asked him slowly.

"I love you, Kimberly, and I am not satisfied with living with you without the benefit of a marriage. I respect you too much for that, and if anything should happen to me, I want you to be secure as my wife." His look was pleading.

"What about your arrangement?" she asked him slowly, her heart hammering inside her breasts.

"It's not my arrangement but my father's and there is no way I am going to honor it," he told her soberly. "Marry me, Kimberly, and make me the happiest man in the world."

"I would love nothing more than to do that." She framed his face and rested her head on his forehead. "I love you as well and you do not have to put a ring on my finger for me to know how you feel about me."

"I want to do it," he told her quietly. "I want you to be my wife, to be Mrs. Peter Kamato, to be joined together with you as one, I want it for me."

"You make it so hard to say no," she told him softly. "What if he finds out?"

"Then he finds out," he said grimly. "What do you say?"

"I say yes, although I think it is not a good idea," she told him breathlessly.

"Good," he murmured softly.

"There is only one condition," she continued. "We do not announce this to anyone until after the year is passed. We wait and see what happens. He might change his mind. I do not want to be responsible for you losing the company."

"Done," he said, knowing that he would agree to anything as long as it meant that she was going to be his wife.

"We are really doing this?" she asked, her eyes wide.

"We are." He started unbuttoning the dark-blue shirt she was wearing, pushing it off her shoulders so that it fell to the floor. The shutters were drawn and the only light in the place was a light in her office so no one could see them from outside. She had on a nude-colored bra and her large nipples were stiff against the silk of the material. He unhooked the front clasp and her breasts sprang free for his eager gaze. "I want you swollen with my child," he told her thickly, using his hands to cup her breasts. "I want to see my son or my daughter feeding from them, but first I want to feed from them." He bent his head and pulled on one nipple with his teeth. Kimberly groaned and grabbed his head, tunneling her fingers through his dark springy hair. He was busy unhooking her denims and she stepped out of them leaving only her matching panties. He reached inside it and touched her there causing her to cry out as the desire spiraled inside her. His fingers reached inside her with urgent thrusts and she moved against them, her body swaying against his. He brought her swiftly to her release before pulling out his fingers and taking out his throbbing erection. With a groan, he lifted her up and entered her from behind his hips lifting as he thrust inside her, his hands on her hips as he brought her down on him. Kimberly sobbed as she felt him deep inside her touching the very core of her. He stood up and turned her around so that she was half lying on the desk and holding her hips firm he thrust inside her, his body clenched with the fire burning through him. He felt himself harden even more as her movement became more frantic and her bottom slapped against him. He spilled his seed inside her, his body covering hers and his hands moving to her breasts cupping them as he called out her name again and again!

*****

They confided in her two best friends because they wanted them to be witnesses. They also told her mother who asked them if they were willing to face the consequences of being found out. "We are," they answered at once.

"Then I am happy for you." She hugged hem both. "But because it is a secret, Peter, does not mean it cannot be a proper wedding with cake and something to eat."

It was the first Saturday in April and it was a lovely spring day. Her dress was a lemon-green silk and was fitted at the bodice and flared out at the waist. Her hair was braided in many tiny braids and gathered on top of her head with tiny rosebuds all over. She was wearing a dazzling diamond necklace he had bought her and matching bracelet and she had on matching pale green heels that gave her several inches in height. He wore a black tuxedo with a sprig of tulip in his lapel. She was carrying a bouquet made up of dahlias, tulips, and larkspur, and her makeup was so minimal, it looked like she was not wearing any. The ceremony was performed at a chapel far in the countryside and the wife of the minister provided the musical interlude. Her friends and her mother stood at the altar with them as they said their vows.

In less than two hours, they were husband and wife, and he placed the beautiful diamond solitaire on her finger. They would not be wearing it in public, only whenever they were together.

"I know it will work out," Simone told her, hugging her friend tightly, the tears glistening in her eyes. She had worn a floral dress that looked great against her skin and Deidre had worn a purple dress. "You two are too much in love for it not to work out."

"Thanks." She hugged her back.

"Nothing is impossible as long as you are in love," Deidre told her, kissing her on the cheek. They went back to her mother's place where they had a delicious meal of fried chicken, coleslaw, potato salad, sweet and sour chicken, and beef broth. In the middle of the table, there was a three-tier vanilla icing cake that her mother had made.

"Thanks, Mom," Kimberly said tearfully, giving the woman a hug.

"It's the least I can do," she told her daughter gently. "He is a rare find and no matter what, he is worth fighting for."

*****

He wanted to take her somewhere for their honeymoon, but she had told him she was content staying in the apartment with him and drinking wine and making love by the simmering heat of the fire. Even though it was spring, it was still very cold outside and it had snowed just two days ago.

"My wife," he murmured, pulling her between his legs as they sat watching the flames.

"My husband," she said softly, leaning back against him. "I can't believe it."

"Whatever happens, I will never leave you." He placed his chin on top of her head. "I was wondering if I should have told my mother."

"You think she would have been on our side?" She looked up at him curiously. He had told her what his mother had said to him some months ago.

"She looks preoccupied and happy sometimes, but apart from saying hello to me at breakfast, she never said anything to me again. I feel sorry for her. She is trapped into a loveless marriage and will never get to know what we share," he said heavily.

"You should try talking to her and maybe she would want to meet me someday," Kimberly ventured.

"I will see how it goes. In the meantime, I just want to enjoy my wife and not think about anything else." He turned her around and looked at her exquisite face. "I saw you walking towards me today and I wondered if I was dreaming," he whispered.

"I can assure you that this is very real," she whispered, opening her mouth as he placed his on hers. His hands were gentle as he stripped off her clothes and made love to her to the sound of the wood crackling under the flames.

*****

"When are you going to tell him?" Charles asked her quietly. They were at his house on Thursday afternoon after jazz class, and he had made them supper. He had asked her to marry him and she had told him she could not do it. She could not divorce him.

"Is it about the money?" he had asked her when she told him.

"I have been married to him for over thirty years and I feel that I owe him something," she had told him miserably. Since the night he had been inside her room and told her what he thought of her, she had been feeling more and more that the marriage was definitely over but how could she leave?

"No," she told him now, putting aside the wine glass she had in her hand. "I can't."

"I can't go on like this, Mitsui." Charles came to sit beside her, taking her hands in his. "I am not used to being in a situation like this and it is driving me crazy! I hate sneaking around and that's what we are doing."

"I am going to create a scandal in my family, so forgive me if I need a little time," she told him tearfully. She went home to her unhappy place and left her heart right here with him. She had barely spoken to her son, and whereas they usually have dinner together as a family, that was no longer the case. They were all living separate lives. "I live in a house instead of a home and we are all like strangers passing through. I need a little more time, Charles." She clung to his hands tightly as if they were lifelines keeping her from going under and maybe they were. "You are the only good thing in my life right now, so I am asking you to bear with me a little bit."

She had tears in her beautiful soft black eyes and he did not want to contribute to her misery. He lifted her soft delicate hands to his lips and kissed them tenderly. "Take the time," he murmured. "I am here and not going anywhere."

She snuggled up to him and rested her head on his shoulders, closing her eyes with a sigh but could not help but think that it was rapidly coming to a climax!

*****

Kimberly gazed at her rings for a long time before putting them back into the velvet jewelry box and snapping the lid shut. She was getting ready to go to work on Monday, the first working day after her wedding. He had left her early this morning to go to the office and said he would be back later. Her husband! She hugged the thought to her. She had never met his parents and his father would not approve of her but right now she did not care.

"Don't you think that your father is going to start questioning the fact that you are not at home at all?" she had asked him last night.

"I don't care," he had told her grimly. "I am your husband and I am not going to be sleeping away from you."

He had made love to her then and they had clung to each other.

*****

It was late afternoon while she was dealing with a client about her sick puppy when Brian came to tell her that there was someone there to see her. "I will be right there, Brian," she told him and turned back to the woman as she explained that she had taken the puppy to the vet and there was still no change. "I am wondering if I should change his diet?" the slight, overly anxious woman said to her nervously.

"Maybe you should try that," she told the woman with a smile, squelching her impatience.

It was another ten minutes before she could get away to attend to the person Brian had told her about. He was standing by her office and he had a commanding figure. Before he turned around, she knew exactly who he was and her heart started hammering inside her chest.

"Ms. Gayle," he nodded briefly. "I can see why my son is so fascinated." He looked at her with cool impassionate stare and Kimberly felt as if she had just been touched by ice. "I do not blame him."

"Mr. Kamato." She did not hold out her hand and he did not offer. "How may I help you?" She kept her voice cool and collected, careful not to show any fear. Men like him preyed on people who showed that kind of emotion.

"Is there somewhere private we can talk?" he asked looking around at the small cramped space with a sweeping glance.

She indicated her small office reluctantly, not willing to let him into her space.

"We already know who each other are so I will dispense with the formalities. My son fancies himself in love with you."

"We are in love with each other yes," she told him coolly.

He laughed shortly, causing her to look at him in surprise. He did not look like Peter, but his son had apparently taken his height from him. His face looked cruel and even when he laughed, it did not change the appearance. His expensive charcoal suit although it fitted him well did not give him the elegance and charm his son exuded.

"Love! Such an overused word, don't you think?" He had not taken the seat she had indicated and she did not sit either. "Kamato Holdings is a powerful company and we are a powerful family, Ms. Gayle. You own a business, so to speak," his voice was scathing. "So you have a little idea of what kind of work goes into making a company successful or maybe you don't," he said with a dismissive shrug. "I always get my own way and I have told my son to get this thing with you out of his system or do you think you are worth much more than a billion dollar?" His tone was mocking and his eyes swept over her and left her quivering inside.

"I am worth much more than that, Mr. Kamato," she told him icily. "I love your son and the fact that you have put a monetary value on our love makes me feel sorry for you. This thing that you think we are involved in is going to last so you can either get on board and stop trying to run everybody's life or you can step aside and let us lead ours."

He stood there staring at her for long that she thought about fleeing but she stood her ground. She was not going to show any fear!

"I always win, Ms. Gayle, and I intend to win this one. My son has not a dime to his name and he has been used to being a billionaire and all the trappings of wealth. Let us see if he is willing to take the chance of having that taken from him. We will see how in 'love' you both will be then. Have yourself a pleasant afternoon." With that he left the office, leaving the door open behind him. Kimberly saw when he stopped for a little bit and looked around the store, his bearing one of contempt. Then he looked back at her with a mocking smile before leaving.

*****

She waited until he got home before she told him. He had brought take-out Chinese food and she shared it out on plates. She had showered before he got there and had pulled on a t-shirt and old sweatpants.

"How was work?" he asked her pulling her into his arms. She hugged him tight to her and rested her head on his chest, inhaling the scent of his subtly expensive cologne. Everything about him was expensive and his father as despicable as he had sounded was right; he was used to money and it would be hard for him to do without it.

"Hey." He eased her away from him to tilt her chin and looked at her. "What's wrong?"

She moved out of his arms and sat on one of the sofas and indicated for him to do the same. "I had a visitor today," she told him softly.

"And?" he prompted even though he felt the truth inside him.

"Your father came to visit." She told him word for word what he had said to her.

"He had no right!"He reached for her hands and held on tightly. "I am going to fix this Kimberly." His heart was racing and he was desperate about losing her.

"How?" she asked him softly. "He is right, Peter. He is never going to accept me, he all but said that and you are not going to get accustomed to living like this."

"What are you saying?" he asked her hoarsely.

"I am saying we should be realistic and consider if this is such a good idea." She had to give him a way out.

"Even if I have to get a job as a busboy or to just work alongside you in the store, I am not leaving," his voice was soft and determined. "It will not come to that because I have an inheritance from my mother's parents but I am not letting you go for any reason and I want you to remember that!"

Chapter 8

"You went to her store?" Peter felt like beating the crap out of him and it was due to the fact that he was his father that stopped him. He had not spent the night with his wife, knowing that he had to have it out with him and let him know that he was not afraid of him. He was having dinner and only looked up at him coolly before continuing to eat the meal set before him.

His mother looked up at him startled. "What's going on?" she asked in alarm looking from one to the other.

"Ask him," Peter said looking at his father furiously. He had not seen him at the office for the whole day and assumed he had meetings out but no he was busy harassing his wife.

"What have you done, John?"

"What I am suppose to do." He pushed away his plate and reached for his glass of wine, leaning back against the chair and staring at his son quizzically. "Our son here fancies himself in love with some black girl." His tone was amused. "I can't say I blame him, she is a fine looking piece of flesh."

Peter saw red and he knew that was exactly what his father wanted. He was spoiling for a fight and he was baiting him but he was not going to rise to it. "Watch it, Gather," he said forcing his voice to be cool and detached even though he was burning up inside. "Your prejudice is showing. Kimberly is the love of my life and it is killing you that I have stood up to you and gone my own way. I am not satisfied to be boxed in the way you want me to be and it is burning you up."

"You think you can throw away our family's tradition just because you think you are in love with some woman?" he sneered, his hand tightening on the stem of the glass. "You are not going to throw away the company you worked so hard to help build just for a woman, Peter, I know you better than that."

Peter walked around to face him and stared him down. "That's the problem, Father," he told him coldly. "You don't know me very well, do you? I am not satisfied to sit in a loveless marriage for the rest of my life because it is family tradition. I am going to walk away from the company and you are going to watch me doing so." With that, he turned and went back through the door. Later, they heard his engine as he drove away.

"He is your only son." Mitsui stared at the man she had been married to for so many years. "Can't you just let go of what you hold so dear and embrace him? He is your own flesh and blood John and he is in love, why can't you be happy for him?" She was trembling with despair.

"What do you know?" he asked her cruelly. "You live in some fairy tale world where a man and a woman live happily ever after. It does not work that way, my dear wife. What we have works and it has done so for a long time. These flashes of emotions fade and reality chips in. Your son is going to realize it when the money he has cannot sustain his lifestyle that he has become accustomed to and when he does, I will be right here waiting to rub his face into it."

"Who are you?" Mitsui felt the meal she had just had churn inside her stomach. How could she have endured being married to this man for so long? And why was she still with him?

"I am a practical businessman who has made a vast amount of money to keep his family in fine style and that's what it's all about." He pushed back his chair and stood up, towering over her. "You would do well to remember that." He strode from the room and minutes later she heard when he drove out as well.

Mitsui sat there around the dining table as the maid cleared away the dishes. She smiled her thanks and found the strength to get up and go to her suite. She had never felt so alone in her life and she realized that no amount of money and fine lifestyle was worth staying in a marriage like this, it was time to get out!

She called Charles.

"What happened?" he asked her swiftly.

She told him everything.

"Where is he now?" he asked her and she knew he was referring to her husband. "He left, I don't know where and I don't care. You are right. I cannot stay, it's becoming more and more unbearable living here, Charles, and if it was not for you I know I would have gone off my head."

"What do you want to do?" he asked her gently, his heart going out to her. He felt so helpless but he had to let it be her decision entirely.

"I am going to tell him tonight," she said tremulously.

"Do you want me there?" he asked in concern. He knew her husband had never gotten physical with her or she would have told him but from what he had heard of the man, he realized that he was a control freak and loved having things way. He was not going to take kindly to his son disobeying him and now his wife's betrayal.

"I can deal with it." She took a deep breath. "I love you, Charles."

"I love you too, baby," he told her softly.

Mitsui hung up the phone and looked around the suite she had called home for the past twenty-something years. She remembered the first place they had lived after they had gotten married. It had been a little apartment above the supermarket. She had spent her time fixing it up and making it look like a home, not that he had noticed. He had been bent on making money and driven on buying as much property as he could. She had never worked because he would not hear of his wife working, he was the man and it was his responsibility! The first time he had had sex with her, he had done it clinically and behaved as if it was a duty and maybe it had been for him. It had been her first time and she had lay there trembling before he came inside the room. He had turned off the lights and gotten on top of her and told her to open her legs. Then he had entered her forcefully and when she had cried out in pain, he had stopped a little then continued, getting his release and then getting off her leaving her dissatisfied. It had been the trend between then from there on and when she had gotten pregnant with their son, he had stopped being with her that way. Mitsui had been so relieved and had prayed that he would never come to her that way again. He never did and she found herself wondering where he was finding his satisfaction, not that she cared. She was just glad he had left her alone.

She had never known it could be so wonderful until she had been with Charles and experiencing that with him she knew that she could never go back to the cold emotionless relationship she was currently in!

*****

He went to see her. He wanted to bury himself inside her and take out his frustrations and anger on her body. He had called and told her to shower and meet him at the door naked because he needed her.

She was waiting by the door for him and as she opened the door, her large breasts were slightly damp and inviting and she was wearing nothing but a pair of black heels. He felt his erection growing. She was his outlet and he was glad he had put her up in an apartment so he could come over and vent his frustrations out on her.

"You look so tired and upset." She touched his fierce brow tentatively. She was afraid of him and even though she loved the money he spent on her, she hated his forceful and arrogant manner.

"Turn around," he told her coldly, going behind her and pushing her up against the door.

He released his erection and entered her, pushing inside her to the hilt, ignoring the tiny gasp of pain that escaped her. He grunted as she closed around him and gripping her hips he thrust into her rapidly, his eyes closed in pleasure. He pulled her away from the door and made her go down on her hands and knees and continued thrusting inside her until with a guttural cry he spilled his seed inside her!

*****

Peter got the call while he was in bed with Kimberly. It was a little past midnight and when his phone rang he woke disoriented. He had come home to her angry and pacing until she had calmed him down. They had made love and then fallen asleep. Now his phone was ringing. "Hello?" he cleared his throat to get rid of the sleepiness and wondered who could be calling him at this hour.

"Peter, it's your mother," she said unnecessarily. "Your father has been in an accident and I am here at the hospital."

For a minute, he wondered if he had died and felt the remorse washing over him. Whatever it was between them, he was his father and he had to respect that. "I'll be right there."

"Go, it's okay," Kimberly said to him softly as he turned to her. "Call me and let me know what happens."

He kissed her lingeringly and climbed out of the bed, dragging on some clothes.

She watched him leave and could not help but think that their lives were about to change!

*****

"He is suffering from severe head trauma and he has slipped into a coma," the doctor was explaining to them. "We are hoping to reduce the swelling of the brain before we operate but we just have to wait and see."

"What are his chances?" Peter asked him abruptly.

The doctor hesitated briefly, looking from mother to son then he said, "I am not sure yet, he has suffered severe brain damage from the accident, we can only hope for the best."

They were not allowed to see him so they went back into the waiting room. "What happened, Mother?" he asked as soon as they were seated.

"He was in an accident." She clasped her hands in front of her fighting the guilt she was feeling. She had decided to tell him she was leaving him the minute he came home and was quite happy about it only to get the call. "He was driving too fast and he hit an embankment and the car overturned with him."

"I thought he was at home," he looked at her searchingly, wondering where his father was coming from so late.

"He left right after you did." She looked at her son. "He was very angry because I stood up for you," she said with a slow smile. "He stormed out."

"I bet he did," Peter said grimly.

"You were with her," his mother stated.

He looked at her and then made a decision. "We are married. She is my wife," he said briefly.

Mitsui looked at him in shock. She never thought he would go that far. "I wished you would have told me," she told him sadly. What a mess!

"We did not want Father to find out and I did not know where I stood with you." He leaned forward. "I love her, Mother, and I have never loved anyone the way I do her. She is my life and without her, the money, the company means nothing to me."

She looked at him and for the first time saw the passion and intensity on his face. "I want to meet her," she told him. She saw the uncertainty on his face and assured him. "I am not your father, Peter, I would never do or say anything to hurt her."

"Okay," he nodded.

They stayed there waiting to get word until it became dawn before the doctor told them that there had been no change, his condition was still the same. "I suggest you go on home and get some rest and we will call you as soon as we have something to report."

*****

His status had changed. The CEO of the company was incapacitated and he was second in command so it was up to him to step up. He called a meeting of the board as soon as he got to the office. He had gone to Kimberly's to shower and change and tell Kimberly briefly what was going on. "I might be late coming home," he told her as he made to leave.

"Of course ,I understand," she told him, feeling the shift already. For the first time since they had been together, he left without kissing her.

"As you have heard my father has been in a terrible accident and is presently in a coma. I will be sitting in as CEO for the time being until I know what is happening," he told them.

"What exactly does this mean, Peter?" Barrington, a long standing member of the board, asked him.

He looked at the man briefly. "It means I am running things right now and I will need to meet with you individually to iron out some details and to know where we are."

"What if he does not wake up?" the man persisted.

"We will deal with it when and if that happens. Dismissed," he told them coolly. "Barrington, please stay."

Peter waited until the men had filed out of the large conference room before he spoke. "Are you trying to undermine my authority?" he asked the man mildly.

"I am just concerned," the man said with a slight shrug.

"Why?"

"Because you are not as experienced as your father and..." He stopped himself.

"Go on," Peter said softly, leaning back against the chair his father used to sit in.

Barrington McGregor shifted uncomfortably in the soft plush chair. The man was much younger than he was and yet he felt as if he wanted to flee from the room. "Your father has been CEO for many years now and as much as you have been a part of the company since you were a child, I don't think you know what running the company entails. I am just concerned, Peter," he added hastily.

"I appreciate your concern," Peter's voice was calm and cool. "But if you voice those concerns in front of the others again, you are gone."

"What?" The man looked at him in shock. "You cannot do that!"

"Watch me." He leaned forward in his seat. "Your alimony payments are more than you can manage and you have started drinking again. I know a lot about you, Barrington, and I would not hesitate to use it."

There was silence in the room for a spell as the man stared at him furiously. "I thought you were better than your father," he said bitterly.

"I am," Peter told him smoothly. "And I aim to prove it."

*****

"I don't get to see you," Charles complained as she picked up her pocketbook getting ready to leave. It had been three weeks since the accident and her husband had not made a change. She went there every day to sit by his side and read to him because the doctor had told her that it would help if he heard a familiar voice. His phone had rung constantly and when she answered the call at one time, the person had hung up. She had used her phone to call the number and had gotten a young female voice.

"This is Mitsui Kamato, who are you?" she had asked.

The girl had hesitated before saying, "I am a friend of John's."

"You can put it in the right context, my dear; you were sleeping with my husband," Mitsui had told her mildly. "He has been in an accident and I take it he was coming from your place when it happened."

"I am sorry," she had muttered and hung up the phone. She had not called back since.

"I have to be there for him, Charles, you have to understand that. He is still my husband," she protested. She had been torn with guilt and wondered if this happened for a reason. She had gone to the hospital every day since the accident and she felt it was her duty.

"He treated you like dirt and you were planning on leaving him Mits, you don't have anything to feel guilty for."

"Don't I?" she asked him sadly. "I broke my vows to him and now he is in a coma and it happened the very night I was planning to tell him I wanted to leave. What does that say?"

"It says that this is your way out," Charles insisted. "Please don't look at me like that. We are both thinking it. The man was a bastard and made all around him unhappy, so don't expect me to play the hypocrite and be sorry about what happened to him."

"Are you implying that I am a hypocrite?" her voice was icy.

"No Mits, I am not but sadly enough even now that he is incapacitated he is coming between us. I am beginning to think we were not meant to be."

"What are you saying?" she whispered.

"I can't go on like this, just waiting to see what happens," he told her wearily. "Do what you have to do."

She had left and gone to the hospital right after. That had been two days ago and he had not called her.

She lifted her head from the newspaper she was reading to see her son come inside the room. He looked different somehow, more authoritative and sure of himself.

"You don't have to do this every day, Mother," he told her with a brief smile. He had started coming home more and she was still yet to meet his wife.

"The doctor says it will help." She put aside the paper she had been reading and gave him her full attention. He did not sit but stood just inside the doorway looking at both of them.

"Do you really want him to revive mother?" he asked cynically, coming further inside the room.

"Why are you saying that?" his mother asked in alarm, glancing at her husband as if she would see him wake up and answer in his usual harsh manner.

"Because it's the truth." He looked down at the man who had fathered him and had tried to control his life since he came into the world. "He treated us like crap and was coming home from one of his women when he met in the accident."

"You knew?"

"Yes." He glanced at her briefly, his heart turning over for her. "I have known for more than a month now because I needed leverage to use against him. He was always talking about family and values and he was sleeping with a woman young enough to be his daughter."

Mitsui stared down at the hands in her lap. What if he found out about her and Charles? "We did not have a traditional marriage," she reminded him, her gaze going to her husband still frame. "I guess he needed an outlet for whatever it was that he was facing."

"You are generous for a woman that has been cheated on over and over again," Peter said dryly. "Let me know if there any changes." With that he turned and left.

Mitsui sat there looking after him and realized that what her son was directing towards her was utter contempt. How could she have sit at home year after year and let him walk all over her and do whatever he wanted to do? With a shuddering breath, she felt the tears coming!

Chapter 9

"What's going on?" He had finally come home tonight after calling her and telling her he was picking up dinner. She had not seen him since last week and he had told her he was busy with meetings and he needed to go home to be with his mother some nights and she had accepted it.

"What do you mean?" He looked cold an unapproachable, not like the Peter she knew and loved and it scared her. She had gotten home before him and had taken a shower and was in the middle of twisting her thick heavy hair when he came. He had brought Chinese food and a bottle of red wine. She had sat there in the living room while he put the things on the kitchen counter.

He had come to sit in front of her and asked her how her day was and she had asked him the question. "You are in and out and we have not made love in a week, Peter. I need you to tell me what is going on." She piled her heavy hair on top of her head and secured it with a thick rubber band.

"You know what is going on, Kimberly." He avoided her eyes and stood up abruptly. "I am now running a company and my father is in a coma. My mother depends on me for everything now so I have to be there. I have asked you to come and live at the house and you refused. What am I supposed to do?"

"I am not going to live at a place where your father who did not in any way approved of me lives. What happens if he comes out of the coma? What do we do then?" She stood up as well. She had felt him slipping away from her and she could not do anything to stop it.

"What do you want me to do, Kimberly?" He turned around to face her. "I am here now, aren't I? Instead of arguing we should be spending the time making up for when I am not here."

"You think you can make up for when you are not here?" she asked him coldly. "I am your wife, Peter, and I am not some submissive Asian woman from your culture who is prepared to fold her arms and take whatever you mete out to her. I am different and if you don't want to be married anymore just say the word."

He stood there looking at her in frustrated anger and then he strode into the kitchen with her following behind him. "I need an answer, Peter."

He slammed his hands down on the countertop causing her to jump. "I am doing the best I can, why can't you see that?" he asked her tightly, his dark eyes smoldering as he reached for her. "Do you think I want out of the marriage?" He pulled the t-shirt over her head and he stood there staring at her unfettered breasts with their dusky brown nipples. She was wearing tiny black lace underwear. "I need you." He lifted her and put her on the counter, pulling down her panties in the process. "I need you," he repeated as he lifted her legs and dipped his tongue inside her. Kimberly had thought about fighting him but when he touched her, the weakness invaded her body and cutting off every logical thought she had. She gasped and settled back against the counter as his tongue thrust inside her, his teeth grazing her mound. She moaned and put her feet on his shoulders as he continued to dip inside her. He lifted his head from her and stood there staring at her moodily before undressing hurriedly. He was fully erect and with a moan he lifted her off the counter and placed her on one of the stools, entering her immediately. "I need this, I cannot get enough, so don't ask me if I want to end the marriage, never ask me that." He finished the sentence with a tortured groan and started moving inside her, his lips on her nipple. She wrapped her legs around his waist and met his thrusts urgently, her body trembling against his. She had missed him so much and hated being without him for even a night.

"Give me a child." He had lifted his head and was looking at her, his dark eyes unreadable.

"What?" She shook her head to get rid of the fog of desire clouding it.

"I want to see you swollen with my child," he told her, gripping her hips thrusting deep inside her causing her to gasp and moan.

"No," she tried to sound firm and resolute but her voice came out shaky and trembling. He had slowed down his movements and pulled out of her, resting the tip of his penis on her mound and rubbing against it, making her almost out of her mind with need.

"Please," he muttered hoarsely. She watched as he held his erection, wet from her insides and rested it against the edge of her opening. "Say yes," he demanded, slipping inside her a little at a time and driving her crazy.

"We can't." She was trying to fight the fire licking at her but it was hopeless. "We are not ready."

"Tell me yes," he commanded, and with a sudden force he entered her fully, lifting her off the stool and holding her hips steady while he thrust inside her urgently. Kimberly wrapped her arms around his neck and bit down on his shoulder hard causing him to jerk against her! He came inside her with such force that he had to sit back on the stool with her on him as he spilled his seed inside her helplessly, crying out her name brokenly. She came in the middle of it and he fused their mouths together, their bodies shaking as they clung to each other.

*****

That night while they were in bed, they laid there both caught up in their own thoughts. They had attempted to eat the food but he had reached for her in the middle of ii and they had made love again up against the wall, afterwards he had sucked her dry, going down on his knees before her.

"Why do you want a child so badly?" she asked him quietly.

"I just want one, that's all," he told her briefly. "We are married so the next step is to have children."

"I see." She eased up and rested back against the mound of pillows against the bed. "I don't have a say in it?"

"Don't you want children?" He turned his head to look at her, taking in her beautiful skin and her breasts that make him ached with desire every time.

"I want children when we are doing it for the right reason, Peter, and somehow I am thinking that you do not want it for the right reason." She looked down and felt her heart ached. These days it was only when they were making love that she felt close to him. What was happening to them?

He shrugged his shoulders eloquently. "Suit yourself." He turned onto his side and turned out his light. "Get some sleep."

Kimberly fought the tears and taking a deep breath she turned out her light and moved as far away from as possible remembering when they used to cuddle up and sleep in each other's arms.

*****

"You look like hell," was the first comment from Brian as soon as she went in the next morning. Peter had left very early with a chaste kiss on her forehead telling her he would see her later. She had stayed there in bed after he had left and wondered if they had made a mistake. She loved him that much she knew and she knew he loved her as well, but she was wondering at the change in behavior sine he had taken over the company, he had told her he was prepared to walk away from it and secretly she had wanted him to, except now he was working so hard at proving himself that she was afraid he was slowly slipping away from her.

"Thanks," she murmured going straight to her office. She bit off a resigned sigh as she saw that he had followed her. She took off her spring jacket to reveal a stunningly simple floral dress with a wide skirt.

"Is that new?" he asked her in admiration noticing how the bodice fitted her snugly and how tiny her waist looked in it.

"Don't you have work to do?" she asked him impatiently.

"Not yet." He took a seat in front of her desk. "I cleaned out the cages and put in fresh water so I am free for the next fifteen minutes. Asian delight giving you problems?"

"Who?"

"Your billionaire boyfriend," he said impatiently. "I saw his picture in the papers just recently saying that he had taken over the company from his father and his father was in a coma. How does it feel to be going out with a billionaire?"

"I have no idea," she told him coolly. They still had not made it public that they were married and it was starting to wear on her nerves. "I am dating the man and not his money."

"If you say so." He looked at her searchingly. "I might be out of line for saying this but you don't look like the Kim I knew. The happy go lucky, don't give a rat's ass about anything kind of girl I always admired and wished I could meet someone like her. Whatever it is that's making you so troubled you need to consider if it is worth it." He stood up and ran a hand over his faded denims. "I think I have meddled into your affairs enough for the morning, I will now go and do what I am paid to do." He left her there in deep consideration.

*****

"I have lost who I am and what I am about and it took Brian reminding me for me to realize it." She dug into her garden salad. They were having lunch at a restaurant near to the store and she had left Brian in charge until she returned.

"Brian is an idiot," Simone said mildly, drinking her iced tea gratefully. The spring day was unseasonably warm and balmy and they were in fact expecting a thunderstorm later in the night.

"He has a lot on his plate, Kim," Deidre reminded her friend, referring to Peter.

"A lot on his plate that he will not open up and talk to me about." Kimberly crunched on the lettuce with lack of interest. "We are married and he is intent on going about everything all by himself."

"You are making me have second thoughts about marriage," Simone murmured. She was going to be finishing the school year and packing up and moving to Tulsa in July. "You guys are so in love and now look what is happening."

"But that's just it," Deidre said. "There is no guarantee that every day is going to be good. You have to be there for him, Kim, and try and understand what he is going through."

"He was never close to his father so I do not understand the need to seek his approval even though he does not have a clue as to what is happening around him," Kimberly said with a shake of her head.

"Have you been to visit?" Simone asked her.

"He has never suggested it to me and I don't think I want to go."

"Why don't you take charge?" Simone suggested. "The old Kim I knew would not ask but would just do. Bring back the old Kim."

*****

"Honey, you look tired," her mother exclaimed as soon as she saw her. She had called and told her that she would be coming over for dinner. She had been putting Peter's needs before hers and when she knew he was coming over she would be at home waiting for him, that's all going to change now.

"I have not been sleeping too well." She placed her pocketbook on the counter and sniffed the air. Her mother was making pot roast and the smell had hit her as soon as she came through the white picket fence. She had noticed that the garden was rioting with spring flowers and the scent had been competing with the smell of her mother's cooking.

"Are you by any chance pregnant?" There was a hopeful note in her voice as she looked at her daughter.

"You are as bad as Peter," Kimberly said dryly, taking an apple from the dish on the counter.

"So I take it that's a no?" she teased.

"A definite no," she said firmly. "We have not sorted out our situation, Mom, and I would never want to bring a child into this confusion."

"Give it time, honey," Karen told her sympathetically. "He is going through a rough patch right now, you just need to be there for him."

"I am trying mom, but he's making it hard." She took the salad bowl and went with her mother to the dining room.

*****

She had not told him she would not be there and when he went inside he was surprised to find the place in darkness. He had left a little late because there had been a meeting that had ran over. His father was used to doing things his way, but he was implementing some changes in the company where the board members had more say to what goes on in the business.

He had come home at seven-thirty expecting her to be waiting for him and was surprised she was not. He knew he had been holding himself aloft from her but he had so many things churning inside him that at times he felt as if he was going to burst right open. He watched his mother go to the hospital faithfully each day and had stopped asking her why. She was free to do whatever she wanted to. He dialed her number and it went straight to voice mail. Where the hell was she?

He took a shower and made a sandwich from some lettuce and cheese he saw in the fridge and was reminded of the first time he had been invited to have dinner with her and she had told him that take-out was her best option because she was not into cooking. He wandered around the room, picking up a t-shirt she had left on the sofa, inhaling her scent of some flowery body wash. She had asked him if he wanted out of the marriage and he had felt himself getting scared. He could not lose her but he also could not stop himself from keeping her at a distance. As long as he did not know where he stood in the company he could not relax. What if his father woke up tonight or even in the morning? Every time his phone rang he was expecting to get a call telling him to get out of Kamato Holdings and never return. He had told Kimberly that he was willing to walk away from it and he had also told his father that as well, but was he?

He glanced at the clock with a frown noticing that it was almost eight-thirty and dialed her number again, but it went straight to voice mail. He was just about to call her friends when he heard the key turn in the lock and she came in. He sat there while she took off her jacket and hung it up revealing the dress she was wearing. She was stunning! He never got used to it, no matter how many times he saw her. "Where were you?" he asked her softly.

"I was at my mom's," she answered, looking at him briefly before going into the kitchen to put a container on the counter. "Are you hungry? She sent over pot roast for you."

"Thanks, I ate a sandwich." He had followed her inside the kitchen. He blocked her exit as she made to leave the room. He had put on a loose bottom and his upper body was bare, his chest smooth and finely muscled. "I called you twice and your phone went straight to voice mail."

"My battery died." She looked up at him with a level stare.

He stood there staring at her and she returned the stare without flinching. "I have been pushing you away because of how mixed up and confused I am, please forgive me."

"Okay." She nodded.

He took her shoulders and brought her closer to him. "I don't want to lose you," he murmured huskily. "Please bear with me, I cannot lose you."

"You won't."

*****

That night he made love to her so tenderly that it left both of them shivering with need. He undressed her slowly, kissing every exposed inch of her body and had her so fired up with desire that she could not keep still. It was then and only then that he entered her slowly, his movements measured as he thrust inside her, holding her to him tenderly, kissing her face and holding her to him for the entire night.

*****

She rushed into his arms and he held her tightly. She had called him and told him she was coming over and he had told her yes. She had decided not to go to the hospital tonight because she wanted to be with Charles. Her husband's condition was still the same and she was tired of wondering if he was going to wake up and what would that mean.

"I am glad you came." He hugged her tightly, lifting her into his arms he carried her off to the bedroom where he laid her down gently on the bed. He had told her that he could not continue like this, but the past few days he had not heard from or seen her had been very hard on him. For now he was going to take what he could get.

"I missed you so much," she murmured, opening her arms to him. He climbed on top of her and entered her gently, feeling her close around him tightly. His big frame shudder on top of her and he took her lips with his in a tender yearning kiss and as she moved with him, he knew he could never let her go!

*****

She went to the hospital without telling him. They had spent the night cuddled together and he had made love to her early in the morning telling her that he would be coming back later.

She gave her name at the nurses' station and was told that his wife was in there with him. She stood at the doorway and watched the petite woman sit there on a chair, a newspaper in her hands. She looked up as she sensed her presence and stood up.

"Hi my name is..."

She did not get any further because to her surprise the woman came forward to meet her with open arms. "You are Kimberly Kamato, Peter's wife."

She looked at the woman in surprise. "He told you about me."

"He did." She glanced around at her husband and instinctively she saw the fear there.

"How is he?"

"Still the same." She squeezed the girl's hands. "Do you mind if we go and get some coffee?"

"Of course."

*****

"I told Peter I wanted to meet you, but I guess he is trying to protect you from the unpleasantness of the situation." She stared down into her coffee, her expression pensive.

"Peter needs to stop deciding what is good for me," Kimberly said dryly. "I know I just met you, but I have to ask you something. Why do you stay?"

Mitsui looked up at the exquisitely beautiful black girl with her sense of independence that she wore like a shroud around her.

"I stay because I am duty bound to do so," she said with a sad smile. "There has been no love lost between us and I had gotten used to the way he treated me which of course is very sad. I was getting ready to tell him I was leaving when he had the accident."

"Oh my," Kimberly exclaimed. "I am so sorry. And now you feel guilty about that," she added shrewdly.

"Please don't tell my son," she pleaded. "I was not only leaving him, but I have fallen in love with someone and I want to be with him."

Kimberly stared at the small beautiful woman before her and realized that she must be suffering so much. "Happiness is fleeting and I understand that he is your husband. I want you to grab that happiness with both hands and don't feel guilty about it."

Mitsui reached across the table and held Kimberly's hands briefly. "I am so happy I get a chance to meet you."

"So am I."

Chapter 10

John Kamato died the 30th of May without waking up. Both Peter and his mother were there. He died in the late afternoon just as Peter got there from work. He had been in a coma for a month and a half.

He left his mother and the doctors in the room and went outside in the waiting room to make a call. "He is gone," he told Kimberly abruptly. They had been getting along tentatively and he had finally confided in her about what he was going through. Some nights she would wake up to find him still awake and staring up into the ceiling.

"I thought you could walk away from the company?" she had asked him with a frown.

"It's the not knowing that is killing me." He turned to face her. "I have made some positive changes to the place, baby, and I know if my father wakes up he is going to go back to the old ways just to spite me."

"It's going to work out," she had assured him.

"Do you want me to come over?" she asked him now. She had her hands full with some new clients and their pets but she would if he wanted her to.

"No I will see you later. We are talking to the doctors now and we are going to be making arrangements for funeral."

"Come home when you are done," she told him softly.

"I will."

*****

Kimberly hung up and took a moment to consider. The man had been her father-in-law and learning of his death she had felt nothing but relief. He had held their lives in his hands and now they were free to what they pleased. She had told him about meeting his mother at the hospital and he had looked at her contemplatively for a moment and then nodded, saying he was happy they had met. She had not told him about her mother wanting to leave and that she had met someone.

The man had been a menace and a stumbling block to all of them so she was not going to pretend she was sorry he was gone.

*****

Mitsui stared at the man she had known and been married to for most of her life. Even in death he looked arrogant. She had asked them to let her look at him before they put the sheets over him. He was gone and he had never spoken a kind word to her or even told her he appreciated her not even once. She finally left his bedside and walked out to the waiting room. She had not called Charles yet preferring to tell him in person. Her son was on the phone when she got there and he hung up when he saw her. "How are you?" he asked her briefly noticing that there were no tears.

"I was used to him always being there so it's kind of strange to know that he is gone," she said with a sad smile. "And I am afraid that I am not regretting that he is gone."

"Neither am I," Peter said grimly. "Let's get out of here."

*****

He had to deal with the Hiroshi's about the arrangement they had with him marrying their daughter. Luke Hiroshi was furious that he was not going to honor their combined wishes. "You had an arrangement with my father, Mr. Hiroshi, and his death has now made that agreement null and void." He had come over to the house as soon as he had heard the news of John Kamato's death.

"So what am I supposed to do now?" he asked in a belligerent tone. He was very small and stocky and his face had turned red with anger.

Peter wanted to tell him that he did not care but he took a deep breath and realized that the man was irate for a reason. "Make new arrangements. Your daughter is a nice girl and would make a suitable wife for someone else but not me. I am truly sorry."

The man turned on his heels and walked away.

"You handled that very well," his mother said coming inside the room. They had not too long come from the hospital and she had gone and taken a shower.

"Thank you," he told her quietly. "I promised Kimberly that I would be home tonight, are you going to be fine by yourself?"

"Why don't you invite her over?" Mitsui suggested impulsively. "That is if you don't mind."

"I will call and ask her," he said quietly, his expression unreadable.

"Do you know he was going to change his will?" she asked him as he turned to leave.

"I suspected," Peter said with a grim smile. "How did you find out?"

"I saw some documents in his office." Mitsui sat on one of the sofas and folded her arms. "He did not keep anything locked away because to his thinking, I am a woman and I did not really understand any of those legalities. He had papers drawn up ready to take to the lawyers, the night before he had the accident. He was doing it out of spite." She raised eyes quite like his own to his. 'The original will leaves everything to you and an allowance for me. It also states that if I got married again I was to be given a million dollars in cash and I should vacate the premises immediately."

"What a charming man," Peter said scathingly.

"I have met someone, Peter," she told him and saw the shock on his face. "I was going to tell John that I was leaving him the night of the accident because life is too short for me or anyone to be living the way we lived and I was not going to miss out on my chance of being happy."

"I would like to meet him." Peter sat beside her and took one of her small hands in his. He was thrown a curve about what she had told him but did not feel one ounce of resentment, she deserved some happiness in her life.

"I would like that," She said with a tremulous smile. "Go and call your wife."

*****

He gave her the tour as soon as he brought her back to his place. Mitsui had embraced her and after talking to her for a little bit she went upstairs to her suit of rooms.

"How are you?" Kimberly looked at her husband quizzically. They were in his bedroom and he was undressing her slowly.

"I am relieved that he is dead." He paused what he was doing and looked down at her. "Is that bad?"

"He was a tyrant and I only met him once," She murmured. "Your mother suffered the most I think. I am glad she told you about the man she is in love with. It must be so romantic to fall in love at this stage in her life."

"She is not a doddering old woman, Kimberly," he told her in amusement, lifting her chin to look at her face. "I am so glad I met you," he said soberly. "I saw the way they lived and even when I was a little boy I saw how unhappy she was. I was prepared to settle because I never knew better. I want to ask you something."

"Go ahead." She held on to his hand.

"Will you marry me again? This time with a wedding for everyone to see?" he asked her tenderly.

Kimberly looked at him in surprise. "Are you sure?"

"I am positive," he said with a smile.

"Then by all means, let's get married again." She clasped her hands around his neck. He lifted her and put her on the bed before joining her, undressing her slowly, his gaze lingering on her breasts.

*****

The funeral arrangements were made there was to be a cremation. The ceremony was very somber and everyone was dressed in black. Mitsui was wearing a black kimono with a veil covering half her face. The board members and staff of Kamato's Holding were present and Peter had closed the company for the day in observance of the founder and former CEO of the company. It was a beautiful June afternoon and there had been rain in the morning but had cleared up by the afternoon.

There was a repast at the house and it was a catered event which ended an hour later.

The lawyer was there and after the people had left he suggested that Peter and his mother come into the den so he could read the will. "You can do it right here, Kimberly is my wife."

The man looked at him in surprise then a slow smile lit his craggy Caucasian face. "Your father thought he had you right where he wanted."

"I know," Peter said grimly. "Go ahead Dave."

"As you know, Peter ,he left the entire thing to you," Dave looked at the papers in his hands briefly. "The controlling interests in the company, the stocks and bonds and this house." He glanced at Mitsui briefly and looked away straight away.

"It's okay Dave," she told him quietly. "I already know what it says about me."

"Ah well yes, Mitsui, I am sorry, I tried to get him to change his mind but he would not hear of it. "He paused and looked at Peter. "He had every intention of changing his will because you would not come to heel. He had the papers all drawn up but did not get to do anything about them because of the accident. So, you are the owner of the company fair and square." He shook his graying head. "For what it's worth and despite the fact that I admired him as a business man, as a human being, he was a complete failure. I beg your pardon," he said with a small cough.

"Never apologize for telling the truth, Dave," Peter told him with a wicked grin. "Thank you."

He left shortly after.

"I want to sell the house," Peter murmured, looking at his wife and then his mother.

"I think you should. You both deserve a new start," Mitsui said with a smile. "And I am telling you both now. After the appropriate mourning period, I am going to marry Charles."

"And I wish you all the best, Mother," Peter went over and clasped his mother's hands briefly.

*****

They were married again on the last day of June at a small chapel nestled in the middle of the woods. She wore white this time, a flouncy white dress that came just above her knees and dangerously high heels that brought her to her husband's chin. He had bought her another set of rings: a princess-cut diamond set that dazzled the eyes. His mother was there as well as Charles and several people from his company. Her friends stood with her at the altar while they repeated their vows.

Afterwards they had dinner at a quaint little inn near to the chapel. He did not have time to go on a honeymoon just then because of the changes in the company, but he promised as soon as he was able he was going to take them somewhere special. She was happy they were not leaving then because she would have missed her friend's departure for Tuscany on the third of July.

They threw her a going away party the night before at the house. She had officially moved over and had given up her apartment. They were going to be looking for an appropriate spot to build their house but in the meantime they were staying at his original home.

Mitsui had left a little while ago and her husband had told her he would be working a little late so they could have their party in peace.

"I am going to miss you," Kimberly told her with a sigh. They had opened the gifts already which ranged from lingerie to cookbooks to an Italian dictionary. "Who is going to intervene between Deidre and me?"

"I am only a phone call away." She was very close to tears. Her students had made her a collage of pictures with all of them on it and she had looked at it and almost broke down right then. Several of the teachers were also there and one of them spoke up, "Who is going to speak up for us for better classrooms and the amount of stationery we are supposed to be allotted?" There was a chorus of agreement which was interrupted by Deidre. "Enough! This is supposed to be a joyous occasion for Simone and I am very happy for her, we all should be."

There was a nod of agreement and from then on the tone of the party changed.

*****

Peter waited until she was sleeping. He went into the study and sat behind the desk that had belonged to his father and switched on the desk lamp. The place was bare and scantily furnished and the desk drawers were locked but he had found the keys in his father's belongings that had been retrieved from the accident. He sifted through the titles and found a notebook with his father's handwriting. It was a list of properties and stocks owned by the company and what had been done to them. His father had been very thorough and precise and left nothing to chance. He had also never trusted anyone and there was a separate list with all the members of the board and their weaknesses. His eyes widened as he came upon the name of one of the board members. He was

Reeves Blagrove and he had the most interest in the company apart from his father and him. He had discovered that Reeves had been selling stocks secretly and had been planning to deal with him. So it was left up to him to do so. He laid aside the book with a tired sigh. Was he going to be able to run this billion dollar company successfully? What if he failed? He was not as single-minded as his father was. He had a wife whom he loved so much that he found himself shaking with the force of that love and he was not prepared to put the company before her.

He heard the movement in the doorway and without turning his head he knew she had come to find him.

"What are you doing?" She moved towards him and sat on his lap. He had neglected to put on a shirt but had pulled on his sweatpants. She was wearing one of his shirts to cover her nakedness. "Just going through some of his things." His hand found its way underneath the shirt and felt her pubic area.

"Are you okay?" She gasped as his fingers dipped inside her.

"I am now," he told her huskily, thrusting inside her slowly, torturing her. He repositioned her to put her legs around him so that she was facing him. He eased her up a little to take out his penis and then he entered her.

"Peter," she moaned, tightening around him. The shirt was opened and he bent his head to capture a nipple while she rode him eagerly her back arched. He pushed away from the desk and held her hips firm, thrusting inside her hard and fast.

"I love you," he cried out, his body trembling. "I love you so much." He lifted her and took her with him back to their bedroom, his penis still buried deep inside her. He closed the door behind them and braced her back against the wall, his thrust seeking and desperate as he brought them both to a stunning and overwhelming release!

*****

Reeves Blagrove was the youngest member of the board aside from Peter. He came from a very privileged family and had been to an Ivy League school. At forty-five, he had been married twice and had no children. He was suave and handsome with thick brown hair and hazel eyes and spent his time working out at the gym inside his pent house suite. He believed in lavish living and had his doting parents to bail him out of every situation he had ever found himself in.

"Hey Peter," he greeted the new CEO warmly. He was not like the other old farts who believed that the younger man was going to bring the company down, he was all about changes and he had always privately thought that John Kamato was an arrogant son of a bitch.

Peter had called him in for a meeting in his office. He had not taken his father's office, preferring to keep his own.

He nodded briefly to the man and handed him a folder.

"What's this?" He opened the folder curiously and read what was in the file swiftly before looking up at Peter. "Where did you get this?" His affable manner had all but disappeared.

"My father had you under investigation for a while now and before the accident was planning on exposing you and having you kicked off the board," Peter told him coolly. "What I cannot understand is why? I thought you were happy here and you wanted to become a part of the company for a long time yet."

"He had no right to do that." Reeves' hazel eyes blazed as he desperately tried to stop the trembling in his arms.

"Oh, but that's where you are wrong," Peter said softly. "He had every right, this company belonged to him."

"What are you planning to do?" His resentment and anger was apparent.

"That's up to you. I noticed that you have sold ten percent of your interests and as a show of good faith I am going to allow you to buy them back and then you are going to sell them back to me along with your other ten percent." Peter's face was impassive and unreadable.

Reeves sat there and felt the sweat around the collar of his shirt. The air conditioner in the office was on full blast but he felt as if he was standing before a blazing fire. "I was in trouble," he muttered. "I owed gambling debts and I was being pressured to come up with the money, I did not have a way out."

"Mommy and daddy were no longer footing the bill?" Peter asked him scathingly.

His face turned red with fury and embarrassment! It was a standing joke among the members of the board and even staff members that Reeves had parents who bailed him out of every situation and that he was not man enough to do it himself.

"I did not want to bother them with this," he said stiffly. "I had no choice."

"We always have a choice." Peter leaned forward in the chair and met his gaze head on. "You have until the end of the week."

"Today is Wednesday," the man protested, feeling his bowels turned to water.

"So, you have no time to waste now do you?" Peter's gaze was dismissive.

Reeves stood up on shaky legs and headed for the door; he turned back to look at Peter but the man was already looking at his computer screen as if he had forgotten that he had been in the room. He was wrong, the son was worse than the father!

*****

He had meetings with all the board members separately and told them that there were going to be changes. He could feel their impotent rage, but he had to make them realize that he was not a push over and that he was in authority.

His mother called him when he was rushing out to a meeting. "Mother, are you okay?" he asked in concern.

"I am fine, Peter," she answered warmly. "Just wanted to know how you were getting on."

"I am okay, Mother." He paused. "How about inviting Charles over for dinner on Saturday?"

"Oh Peter, I would love that!" she exclaimed. "I want to thank you for not judging me and for accepting him. It makes me feel so much better."

"You are welcome," he told her. "I have to rush out to a meeting just now. Will you be home for dinner later?"

"I will," she responded. "See you then."

She hung up the phone and turned to face Charles. She had been spending more and more time with him lately and she could not believe how free and happy she felt. "He wants you over for dinner on Saturday."

"I would love that," Charles told her, wrapping his arms around her.

She rested her head on his solid chest and sighed with contentment. She was finally happy.

Chapter 11

It came unexpectedly. She had gone off the pills because she had been having an allergic reaction to them and had not found the time to go back on something else. She had been so busy with work and with them trying to find the perfect spot to build their home that she had not had the time. Besides that, Mitsui and Charles had planned their wedding date for the second of August, so there was a lot going on.

They were having breakfast one morning; Mitsui had spent the night over at Charles' and had not returned yet, so it was only she and Peter. One minute she was eating the oatmeal with raisins and cinnamon and the next minute she felt the wave of nausea wash over causing her stomach to clench and the sweat to pop onto her forehead.

"Kimberly, what's wrong?" Peter was up in a second as he saw her bent over on the table.

"I think I am going to be sick." She shook out of his hands and raced for the nearby bathroom where she emptied out the entire meal and some. She felt him behind her on the floor and when she was spent he pulled her back against him and rested a damp towel on her forehead. She took deep calming breaths to still her heartbeat.

"Feeling better?" His deep voice rumbled against her cheek.

She nodded. "I think I might be allergic to something," she murmured.

"Or you might be pregnant." He lifted her chin to look at her closely.

"Pregnant?" She frowned as she tried to remember the last time she had had her menstrual flows. With all the up and down she had all but forgotten about it and realized that she had not had any for quite some time. Her eyes widened as she looked at her husband. "I think you might be right," she said slowly.

Peter was elated! He did not want to jinx it by running ahead of himself, he preferred to consult with the doctor first. "Can you stand?" he asked her.

She stood with his help, her feet a little wobbly as she clung to him. Throwing caution to the wind, he lifted her up and twirled her around with a whoop of joy. "I am going to be a father!"

*****

The doctor confirmed it. She was indeed pregnant. "Going on four weeks," Doctor McIntyre told them after had had finished the examination. They had decided to go into work late and Peter had cancelled the early morning meeting he had set to go with her. "I am going to prescribe some iron and vitamins to help with the growth of the fetus, you are a little anemic but don't worry what I giving you will help."

Doctor Ilene McIntyre had known the family since Peter was a child and offered her condolences about his father. "Thank you, Doctor," he told her briefly.

"What about the nausea?" Kimberly asked her.

"I will give you something that will help somewhat."

*****

"So, who do we tell first?" he asked her as soon as they were outside. It was a hot summer morning and she could not wait to get in the cool interior of the vehicle.

"I will call my mom and you call yours," she suggested.

"Good idea," he said with a smile.

Both mothers were ecstatic at the news! Karen was just leaving out to go and take care of some bills but she said that could wait. "How about you come over and we talk?"

"I have to go to the store, remember?" She forced her voice to remain cheerful. She could hear Peter in the background talking to his mother and hear the excitement from her end.

"Honey, are you up for it?"

"Mom I do not have a terminal illness, I am just pregnant and I do have a business to run," she said a little impatiently.

"I will stop by on my way home. I am so happy, honey," she exclaimed.

*****

She went straight to her office the minute Peter dropped her off. She had been hard put not to show her true feelings and the strain of pretending to be happy with him had taken its toll on her.

"Hey you okay?" Brian asked her curiously following her to the office.

"Not now, Brian," she told him abruptly. "I need some privacy." She slammed the door shut behind her.

She was pregnant! She sat on her chair. The irrational fear of child birth had always been at the back of her mind but she had dismissed it thinking that she did not have to contend with that right now. She knew Peter had been saying he wanted children but she had always avoided the subject. She loved her husband, but the thought of getting swollen with his child inside her was not something she was looking forward to! Who was she going to tell? She could not confide in him and his mother was out of the question, they were over the moon about her being pregnant and she had wanted to discuss her feelings with the doctor but she was a family friend and she was afraid somehow they would find out. She could not tell her mother either because she had sound so excited about the prospect of being a grandmother. That only left Simone and Deidre and she knew what they were going to say. With a sigh, she bent her head on her desk, feeling her stomach rumble and realized that she had basically not eaten anything since morning and it was almost noon now.

She was just about to go and get some soup from the nearby eatery when her phone rang. "Hello?"

"Hey! You sound like you lost your best friend. I am still here girlfriend." It was Simone and she realized that apart from a brief call to say that she was settling in, she had not heard from her since then.

"Simone!" She sat back down and felt the first spark of excitement since the day started. "Oh girl, it's very good to hear from you!"

"Leandro is out back trying to mend a fence in the backyard and here I am waiting dinner for him. How are you?"

"I am pregnant," she told her abruptly.

Simone gave an earsplitting shriek that caused Kimberly to move the phone from her ear. "I am going to be an aunt?"

"I suppose so." Kimberly tried to draw from her excitement but she failed.

"You don't sound too thrilled."

"I am not." She heard how it sounded and continued. "Is it wrong of me not to be excited over the news?"

"It depends on why you aren't," Simone said cautiously. "Why aren't you?"

Kimberly searched for a suitable response. "I think I would have preferred it to be much later in life like maybe when I am in my thirties or so. I am just getting to know Peter and with what went on with his father and he had to hide our love and then his death. I just wanted a break from all the drama and for us to get to know each other better. We have not been out on a proper date because he was thrown into running the company. I am scared Simone, and I do not feel anything for this thing inside me."

"Honey, I get what you are saying and that 'thing' inside you is barely a thing yet. As it grows into something I believe you will start bonding and the bond between a mother and a child is something very powerful or so I have been told," Simone assured her.

"I hope so," Kimberly said with a deep sigh. "How are you?"

"I am great!" she exclaimed. "I am learning to press wine and I have officially become a farmer. We go for picnics in the woods and we take very long walks in the mornings. He is a peach, Kim, and I am afraid I keep expecting him to change."

"Just go with it and stop being so fearful," Kimberly told her.

"Look who is talking?" Simone said teasingly. "Why don't you take a week and come over and spend it with us?"

"I doubt that will work, especially now that I am pregnant," she said wryly. "We are looking for a spot to start making our house and Peter's mom is getting married next month."

"Quite a lot going on."

"You can say that again," she said with a sigh.

"Well suggest it to Peter, you are both welcome but please let him know that this is not a pent house suite but a humble abode but the open spaces and the fresh air would do you guys great."

"I will," Kimberly said with a laugh feeling her mood lighten.

"And honey, make some time to go out. You were cheated of the dating part of the relationship because of his father, but now that he is gone there is no longer an excuse," Simone said seriously.

"You are right."

They chatted a few more minutes and then said goodbye.

He called her every chance he got to find out if she had eaten or how she was feeling and she had to force herself to sound as if she was thrilled. "Peter, I am fine, so stop calling," she told him impatiently. She was in the middle of grooming a dog and the smell of the soap she had used had made her nauseous and she was fighting to keep her soup down. She had not told Brian and she had no intention of telling him right now either. "Brian, can you take over please?" She stood and felt herself swaying slightly.

"Peter, I happen to be working here and each time you call me you interrupt what I am doing," she said impatiently going towards her office. She had to be taking deep breaths to fight the nausea.

"I cannot help it. I am an idiot for you right now," he told her softly. "Do you know how I feel, baby? You are carrying my child inside you and there is nothing I would not do for you. I am sorry if I am overbearing, but I am very excited and apprehensive at the same time. My father was a lousy dad and I want to be different and I keep hearing a voice saying to me that I will not be different. I am going to be my father all over."

"You know that's not true," she told him, sitting on the chair behind her desk heavily. "You are a different man from your father and I think you know that as well."

"Thanks, baby, I needed that. Have you eaten?"

"I had some soup, that's the only thing my stomach can take right now," she told him lightly.

"I will buy you all the soup in the world if that's what you want," he told her huskily. "Thank you, baby."

"For what?" she asked him puzzled.

"For carrying my child."

She cried. As soon as she hung up from him, she burst into tears! She knew it was partly hormones but part of it was she felt like the lowest form of human being there was. How was she going to do this? Pretend that she was as excited as he was when she was resenting the child growing inside her? How could she love her husband so much and not love the part of him he had implanted inside her? What kind of a monster was she?

*****

He picked her up at six. He had asked her about getting a car and she had been thinking about it. She still rode her bike on the weekends when she was home but she knew he was never going to agree to it now. "How was your day?" she asked him as soon as he buckled her in.

"Fruitful." He had not moved but used the opportunity to take her lips with his. "I have been wanting to do this all day." His tongue delved inside her mouth and one hand was on her breast. She was wearing a white cotton dress with thin straps and wide skirt and he reached inside her bodice to cup her breast. She gasped as he ran a finger over her sensitive nipple and braced her back against the seat. "Baby." He dragged his mouth from hers and taking one of her hands he placed it against his crotch for her to feel his pulsing erection. She squeezed lightly and he groaned loosening the buckle of her seatbelt and dragging her over to him, his mouth buried on hers. With a muffled groan he put her away from him, his breathing ragged and his hand shaking as he placed them on the steering wheel. "Let's go home," he said hoarsely.

*****

"I can't believe I am going to be a grandmother." Mitsui rushed towards her as soon as the door opened and they came inside. Her beautiful dark eyes were shining with excitement.

"How do you feel, my dear?" she asked.

"Like any other pregnant woman," Kimberly told her, suddenly feeling very tired of keeping up the pretense of being ecstatic.

"What can I do?" the woman asked anxiously, making Kimberly felt like crap.

"I am just going to drink some tea and your son said I should eat something so I will try and do so." She smiled at the woman kindly.

"I will tell Gerard to whip something up especially for you."

*****

He had baby oil in his hands. He had undressed her slowly and with a lack of haste and then he had hurriedly taken off his clothes. Now he was pouring the liquid into his palm. "I want to pamper you," he told her softly.

"Peter you…" She did not get to finish.

"No talking," he ordered huskily. She watched as he knelt over her and massaged the oil into her breasts, his fingers pinching her sensitive nipples. Kimberly gasped and moved against him. He did not make a sound but continued to rub the oil slowly onto her breasts before moving down to her stomach. She was trembling badly and her hands clenched into the sheets, her heart racing and her body on fire. He had reached down to her pubic area and he lifted her legs and had them bent at the knees. He poured more oil into his palm and rubbed the palm over her mound before slipping a slippery finger inside her, rotating it slowly. The sensation was unbelievable! Kimberly thought she was going out of her mind! Her body convulsed as he slipped another finger inside her, using both of them to thrust inside her slowly at first then increasing the speed. He slipped his fingers out and she watched as he rubbed his hand over the length of his erection, his eyes holding hers. He rubbed the tip of it and her eyes were drawn to it as he continued to massage the oil onto it.

"Peter." She was drowning in desire and she wanted him inside her now.

"Tell me what you want," he told her hoarsely, his hand moving over his erection.

She was mesmerized! "I want you," she gasped feeling that if he did not enter her soon she was going to die of need!

"How much?" His voice was soft and erotic.

"Peter, please," she begged.

"How much?"

"So much that if I don't have you I am going to die," She was trembling so much that her breasts were shaking.

"I love you," he told her, his eyes holding hers. "You are carrying my child and I love you so much that I cannot contain it. I have never felt this way about anyone before and it scares the hell out of me! I want to screw you for the entire night and never stop but I am afraid of hurting you."

"You won't, please, Peter," she cried.

He entered her then, guiding his penis inside her and putting her legs onto his shoulders. "Don't move until I tell you to," he told her tightly. He held the edge of his penis and pulled out of her, using the tip of it to move over her mound before entering her again, not fully and then withdrawing, driving her crazy before he entered her fully, lifting her bottom to meet his thrusts, pushing against her to the very core of her.

"Tell me you want me," his voice was a hoarse cry as he pushed inside her over and over again.

"I want you so much." She was shivering, her body lit from within. "I love you Peter, I love you so much!" He lifted her legs and held them as he thrust inside her, his body moving against hers forcefully. His climax was near but he was in no way through with her yet. He pulled out abruptly and bent over her, his mouth seeking her vagina, his tongue flickering inside her, his teeth grazing her mound as he thrust inside her over and over again! He waited until she was on the edge before stopping and putting his penis inside her, his thrusts frantic and needy, matching hers. She clung to him, mindless with desire, her body shaking from the need inside her. A need that threatened to overwhelm her and take her over the edge. They came together, their cries sounding in the room, their bodies molded together as one as they found their release together!

*****

She slept in his arms and even when he had finished making love to her, he had not wanted to let her go. It was as if he could not get enough of her, as if his desire had become more pronounced by the fact that she was carrying his child inside her. His hands had roamed over her body restlessly, lingering on her flat stomach before drifting down to her pubic area where he had started another storm inside her. He had finally drifted off to sleep after he had taken her lips in a savage and a hungry kiss that had started them up again. They were both exhausted but she could not sleep and laid there in his arms with her head against his chest, the despair cloaking her entire being!

*****

He had called his father and told him he wanted to speak with him and he had been told to come over. His parents had paid for the pent house suite he was living in and had gotten him out of trouble since he was a kid. He was their only child and he could see the disappointment on their faces each time he got himself mixed up into something that they had to clean up but he could not stop himself.

His parents were old money and as such they behaved the way old money behaved. They did not flaunt their riches; even the three story house they lived in had been passed down from generation to generation and had been renovated several times to fit the turn of the century. When their son had told them that he wanted to go on his own, they had been disappointed but a little relieved hoping that he would grow up because he was living on his own, it had not happened yet and he was over forty.

James Blagrove looked up as his son came inside the parlor. His wife had retired for the night and he had deliberately not told her that their son had called. At least she would get a good night's rest tonight.

"Drink?" He was pouring a scotch for himself, knowing that he was going to need it.

"Thanks, Dad," Reeves said with forced gaiety, walking over to the liquor cabinet to stand next to his father. He had a combination of both their features. His mother's eyes and mouth and his father's face and height and that combination had made him very desirable to the opposite sex.

"What is it Reeves?" his father asked him mildly.

"I have gotten myself into a little trouble." He drank down the scotch with a grimace.

"What is it this time?"

He told his father what he had done and how he was supposed to buy back the stocks and he was not able to. "I am ruined, Dad," he said with a shaky sigh. "I know I have been a mess and you and mom have to bail me out constantly but I promise you that this is the last time."

"It's not going to happen," James told his son coolly, placing the glass on the counter top.

"What?" Reeves blinked at him stupidly, not believing what he was hearing.

"We have cut you off Reeves," he told his son firmly. "We have been doing that for too many years now and we have realized that you are never going to stop as long as we continue to do so. You are on your own."

"You don't understand, I am in big trouble here." Reeves realized that he was trembling! This could not be happening!

"I am afraid it is son. You need to find your way." He was leaving the room indicating that the conversation was over. "Lock up after you leave."

"Dad, please you have to help me out." He grabbed his father's lounge coat with desperate fingers.

"No and that's final." With that, his father turned and left him alone in the beautifully elegant room, his body trembling with fear!

Chapter 12

He pampered her and she felt like such a hypocrite because she was not feeling the way he was and she was not deserving of such treatment. He made love to her every night and even when they were coming home he would pull to the side of the road and take her there and then. He left the office one mid afternoon and took her home and made love to her until she was exhausted, he could not get enough of her and he apologized but she felt the same way. Pregnancy had kicked her hormones into high gear! She had been at the store one afternoon and had felt such an intense wave of desire that she had to call him. He had come over immediately and had taken her bent over her desk while Brian had gone to walk some of the dogs.

She wished she was feeling a bond to the child growing inside her.

*****

"I need more time." Reeves came into the office after he had called and requested a meeting with Peter. The week had passed and he had expected to hear that the man had come up with a solution to his problems. But he had been following his lack of progress and realized that he had only managed to dig a deeper hole for himself.

"How much?" Peter asked him mildly, noticing how disheveled he looked. His father had called and told him that they were no longer going to be bailing him out of his tough spots.

"Three weeks," he said hopefully.

"Two," Peter countered. "You can always sell me the ten percent now and use the money to get out of your gambling debts, Reeves."

"You have been checking up on me?" he asked him bitterly.

"Someone has to," he told him mildly. "You are a mess and you are sliding downhill fast. Do yourself a favor and go and get some help."

"I don't need you telling me what to do," he said with a sneer. "I will draw up the papers for the sale."

"Good," Peter said with a nod.

"You think you are so high and mighty because your daddy died and left you a company to run?" The man's eyes were bloodshot indicating that he had been drinking.

"I don't think that at all and I am going to give you some free advice. You are heading into a road that has no way out and before you go down that road too far, I suggest you ask for help," Peter told him mildly.

"Screw you! I don't need your help." With that he left the office, banging the door behind him.

Peter called security and advised them of the situation, asking them to make sure he exited the building without harming himself or someone else.

He sat back in his chair and stared across the room contemplatively wondering if he had done the right thing.

*****

"Okay fine. If this is what it takes to get big boobs them I am in. I am going to get me a man and get pregnant," Deidre said staunchly. They had not met for lunch for the past three weeks because their schedules had been so hectic. She and Peter had found the perfect spot to build their house and construction was starting next week. In the meantime, she had been sick every morning and her husband had been there to hold her head and wiped her mouth but she was still not liking it.

"Be careful what you wish for," Kimberly told her dryly, pushing the spoon around in her soup.

"Oh honey, still nothing yet?" Deidre asked her in concern. Simone had called her and told her to look out for their best friend as she was not in the best frame of mind.

"The only good thing about this is that it has drawn Peter and I even closer," she admitted.

"Don't you think that you should tell him?"

"Tell my overly excited husband that I don't think I want the child we made together?"

"I see your point." Deidre put down her fork and reached for the girl's restless hands. "A lot of people would say you have it pretty good. A handsome and extremely rich husband and one who dotes on you and would do anything for you but sometimes that's not enough. What exactly are you afraid of, Kim?"

"I am afraid of losing him and then end up stuck with a kid that I have to bring up by myself. I am afraid of being a lousy and disappointing mother and I wanted to be able to spend a few years with my husband just getting to know him."

"I can tell you that those are irrational fears but I am no expert in that department. You are going to have to talk to someone, girlfriend. If not your husband then someone else." Deidre squeezed her hand reassuringly.

*****

"I thought you said it was going to be a very small wedding," Charles said looking at her indulgently. Mitsui was practically living with him now. They did everything together;, taking long walks, cooking meals together and even shopping with each other. She was like a kid set loose in the candy store. She had gotten a taste of freedom and she was like a whole new person. When she was not discussing the wedding she was talking about her upcoming grandchild.

"I lied," she told him teasingly, poking her tongue out at him. He could not believe that she was the same person who had been terrified of even her shadow. His death had freed her and Charles' love had matured her into the person she was supposed to be.

"How about daisies and carnations for the decoration?" she asked him, tapping her pencil against her still smooth cheek. She had cut her hair and it now swung against her cheeks in dark waves giving her a pixie look. It suited her and made her look a lot younger and she had said she wanted to shed her past as much as possible.

"You are running the show, my love" He kissed the top of her head and looked down at her list. He had noticed that she put everything in writing and was very organized. "No Japanese wedding?" he teased her.

"I had one and it was a disaster," she told him looking up at him, her hand holding his. "This time it is going to be an American wedding."

He pulled out a chair beside her and took her tiny hands inside his. "You know that I love you very much, don't you?" he asked her seriously. She nodded.

"And you also know that I would never do anything to hurt you?" She nodded again.

"Your husband before is dead and buried and we are starting a new life together. We are going to start fresh without all the hang ups of the past and I promise you that we are going to be very happy together."

"I know," she told him softly. "You made me experience something I have never experienced before: love and happiness and desire. You make me feel beautiful, Charles, and for that I will always love you."

"I never thought I would be blessed to find love again and I did with you." He lifted her up and set her on his lap, cradling her small body with his. She put her arms around his neck bringing his head down for a kiss. Charles lifted her and carried her into the bedroom and for the next hour or so the wedding plans were shelved for the time being.

*****

"Mom, I assure you that I am well taken care of by Gerard," Kimberly protested as her mother plied her with several containers of foodstuff. She had left work early and stopped by her other to visit. She was on summer break but was volunteering at the community center to help kids who needed to get their GED.

"Indulge me," her mother murmured. "I am not going to be able to contribute much to my grandchild seeing as how you are married to a billionaire," she said with a raised brow. "So, I will do what I can now."

She had thought she could confide in her mother but she was so excited that she hated to put a damper on her high spirits. As Deidre said before, it was bound to past.

*****

He was desperate! The two weeks had almost passed and he still had not come up with the money. He had sold his shares and had used the money to gamble in a desperate attempt to solve his existing problems and he had lost! It was the bastard Peter's fault, he raged! Now he owed loan sharks a quarter of a billion dollar as well as trying to come up with the money to buy back the stocks he had sold. He was in big trouble and he was surprised that he had not been slapped with a lawsuit. The only way a stock could be sold was to another member of the board and it had to be approved of by all the members of the board, that had been the only way James Kamato would have allowed his company to go public and he had committed the unpardonable sin by selling his shares to an outsider and used off all the money. He had called his mother this time and cried over the phone and she had told him that she could not help him. They had all turned against him! But he was going to change that, he was going to give them something to regret.

*****

Peter was working late. He had sent a driver to pick up Kimberly from the store because he had meetings he could not get out of and there was the problem with Reeves. He had met with the board to decide on a plan of action. The man was unraveling and there was no doubt about it and his avenues of getting money had all being cut off, there was no telling what he was desperate enough to do.

"Are you home?" He called her phone. He wanted to be there with her. Ever since he had discovered that she was carrying his child, it was like he wanted to be around her for the entire day, every day.

"Just got in now," Kimberly told him. "When are you going to be finished?"

"I have to review some reports for a meeting first thing in the morning and then I will be there. Is Mom there?"

"No," she responded. "I'll be fine. The household staff is here and I am planning to sweet talk Gerard into making me something delicious. For some reason I feel for something spicy."

"You are not supposed to start craving until much later," Peter told her with a laugh.

"Tell that to your child growing inside me," she said dryly.

"Say that again," he demanded huskily.

"What?"

"My child growing inside you," he murmured seductively.

"Peter..."

"Please, baby ,say it again," he pleaded.

"Your child is growing inside me," Kimberly whispered. "Peter, what are you doing?"

"I am hard for you," he told her hoarsely. "My cock is straining against my pants and I have to release it."

"Peter," she moaned, trembling.

"Touch yourself down there," he urged her. "I am running my hand all over my erection and pretending I am entering your wet warmth. Are you wet for me, Kimberly?"

"Yes," she said faintly, the blood pumping through her veins.

"I am inside you now, can you feel me? My teeth are latching onto those delicious nipples of yours and I am stroking inside you with my penis. Can you feel me?"

Kimberly sat on the bed, her body weak. How can he do that to her from such a distance, she thought, feeling her nipples tightened painfully. "Come home, Peter," she said huskily. "Please."

"Soon, baby. I am coming inside you now and you are coming with me." He was breathing fast in her ear and she closed her eyes as she felt his touch on her skin. With a cry, she felt the release flooding through her body!

*****

He barely had time to bring himself under control when he heard the stirring in the outer office. It was a little after seven and he was just finishing up to go home when he heard the footsteps. He knew he was alone in the building except for the guard downstairs and called out to him. "I am just finishing up here, Smith, give me a few more minutes."

"Your time is up," a soft voice told him just inside the doorway. Peter's blood froze as he witnessed the disheveled man standing there with a gun pointed on him. It was a Reeves he had not seen before. He looked like he had not slept in days and his clothes hung off him and made him appear thinner than he actually was. His usually immaculate hair stood on end as if he had been combing his fingers through it constantly.

"What are you doing, Reeves?" he asked him in a calm enough voice. He was standing around his desk and although his phone was on the desk, he knew if he made any sudden movement he would be shot. His only chance was to try and reason with him.

"You ruined my life!" he shouted, spittle flying from his mouth and Peter had no doubt that he had been drinking before he came. "People are looking for me to kill me and it's all your fault."

"You did it all on your own, Reeves." Peter's voice remained calm. "You have a gambling problem and you need help. We can get you the help you need."

"Oh, now you want to help me?" he sneered, coming further inside the room. "It's too late for that, buddy. You think you are so high and mighty because your daddy left you a company and loads of money? You think you are any better off than me? You ruined me! You and my parents, cutting me off like I am some child you can control. But I showed them and I am going to show you."

"What did you do, Reeves?" Peter felt the alarm going through him.

"That's for you to find out or maybe not." With that he raised the gun and fired off a shot!

Peter felt the bullet pierce his skin and found himself falling as if in slow motion. The pain was excruciating! He barely saw the man flee from the office and the only thought inside his mind was that he was dying and leaving his wife and his unborn child. "Kimberly," he whispered before blessed oblivion took over.

*****

Kimberly showered and put on her nightgown. She had persuaded Gerard to prepare something for her and he had made her spicy chicken with a small bowl of rice which she had eaten off entirely. "You are the best!" she had told him with a smile as she went off to her suite.

It was approaching eight-thirty when she started getting worried. She dialed his number and it went to voice mail. "Peter Kamato, where the hell are you?"

She waited a next half hour and was about to dial his number again when her phone rang and his name came up. "You are in so much trouble!"

"Is this Mrs. Kamato?" a strange voice asked her.

"Yes, this is she." Kimberly felt her blood freeze. He was all right, he probably just lost his phone; she told herself in panic.

"I am afraid there has been an accident and your husband is on his way to the hospital," the person said quietly.

"What kind of an accident?" her voice sounded strangled.

The person hesitated briefly. "Could you meet us at the hospital?"

"What's wrong with my husband?" she demanded.

"He has been shot," the male voice told her softly.

"No." She shook her head, her hand gripping the phone. "My husband is at the office, there has been a mistake."

"Is there someone you can call to take you?"

"I…my mother," she said in anguish.

"We will meet you there."

*****

She called her mother and his and they met her at the hospital. There were policemen milling around the waiting room and approached her as soon as she came in. "My husband?" She was shaking so badly that she could hardly stand.

"Take it easy, Mrs. Kamato," a big burly police officer told her kindly, leading her towards a vacant chair. Her mother and Mitsui and Charles were right behind. "The doctors are with him now."

"What happened?" It was Charles who asked the question. The police officer looked up at him and then back at her. "He is family," she said briefly.

He told them what happened and how they had found Reeves Blagrove downstairs with gunshot wound to his temple. "He was a member of the board of your husband's company. Did you know him?"

She shook her head numbly.

"I know him and his parents," Mitsui spoke up."We had dinner together a few times when my husband was alive. Why would he want to hurt my son?"

"We are still investigating, ma'am, but as far as I can tell it seems to be a grudge he had against your son. I spoke to his parents and they said that he had called and had been asking them for money," the detective told her.

"I need to see him," Kimberly said abruptly jumping up. What did it matter why he did it?

Just then the doctor came out pulling off the cap he had on, his face bathed in sweat.

"Mrs. Kamato?"

"Yes?" Both Kimberly and Mitsui answered automatically. "She is his wife." Mitsui pointed to Kimberly.

The doctor nodded. "Your husband is a very lucky man and is also a fighter. The bullet went straight through without touching any major arteries. He lost a lot of blood but he is going to be okay."

Kimberly reached out and gripped his arms. "May I see him?"

"He is resting now but you may go in," he said with a gentle smile, patting her hand briefly.

*****

He looked so still and pale against the white pillows and her heart turned over as she saw the large white bandage just above his heart. He was not dead and that was what she had to hold on to, not matter how much her body trembled when she thought of how he could have died! He could have died leaving her and his child to go on without him and that had been one of her greatest fears! Could she have done that? Was it on her that she had transported her fear on him? She had heard somewhere that thoughts were very powerful and could be put into actions. She pulled up a chair beside the bed and took his hand in hers. She lifted his hand to her cheek and rested her head against it wearily. "You promised you would not leave me and you almost did," she murmured. "If you had died, Peter Kamato, I would never have forgiven you. How would you expect me to bring up a child all by myself?"

"I am still here," his voice sounded weak and tired as he teased her.

She turned her head and met his intense dark eyes. "Peter," she tried to say something but the tears clogged her throat.

"Hush, baby," he said quietly, his hand gripping hers slightly. "I am sorry."

"You ought to be," she told him, her voice trembling. "How do you expect me to go on without you?"

"I called out your name when he shot me," he told her quietly. "I kept seeing your face as I went in and out of consciousness." He winced a little as he moved.

"Stay still," she told him huskily. "I love you, Peter Kamato, and if you ever put me through that again I am going to strangle you with my bare hands."

"Yes ma'am." He smiled at her tenderly.

Chapter 13

He was released from the hospital a week later. Kimberly did not leave his side while he was in the hospital recuperating. She slept on a cot in his room. "Baby, you are pregnant and we have a giant king-sized bed at home, as a matter of fact several beds, please go home, I am fine," he pleaded with her.

"Not a chance buster," she told him firmly, adjusting the pillows behind his head. She had shaved him this morning and sponged him down, refusing to let the nurses do it. "You are my husband and I will be the one doing the touching."

He woke up one night to see her curled on her side and fast asleep on the cot. He knew she had been scared and thought she had lost him that was why she refused to leave. She had been into her store for a few hours each day and had left his mother to baby sit, telling her not to leave until she got there. He had gotten the news of Reeves' suicide and had spoken to his parents who had tearfully told him how sorry they were.

He had thought he was a goner and he had been given a second chance and from now on he was going to spending a lot of time with his wife and their baby when he or she came.

His mother wanted to put off her wedding due to what happened but he had insisted that they went along with it. "Too much has happened mother," he had told her quietly. "It made me realize how short life is and we need to live it and be happy while we can."

*****

She made sure he was comfortable in the bed, instructing one of the maid's to get some fruits from the kitchen and glasses of water. His mother and hers had been by for a visit and also Debbie as well.

"Sit." He patted the bed beside him. The large bandage had come off, leaving a smaller one, and his color had returned. A lock of his hair had fallen down on his forehead and she realized that he needed a haircut. "How are you?"

"I am fine," she told him, sitting down carefully afraid that she was going to hurt him. "I just need to get you something to eat."

"We have people to do that. I need you to talk to me." He looked at her quizzically. He had noticed that she did everything to avoid being near him. She had slept on the couch and told him that she was getting up all the time to go to the bathroom and did not want to disturb him. She was avoiding him. "Talk to me, please."

"We will talk when you get better," she said with a bright smile getting ready to get off the bed. "We have your mother's wedding next Saturday and you need to be well enough to walk her up the aisle."

"Stop." His voice was abrupt and he saw her wince. "Talk to me, Kimberly." No matter what, he never shortened her name like the others did and she suspected he wanted to be different.

"What do you want me to say?" She turned to him and he noticed that there were tears in her beautiful dark brown eyes. She was still not showing and she had done something to her hair. It was braided very small and caught up in a pony tail away from her face. He knew she twisted it every night before going to bed and coiled it around her head and wondered how she managed the heavy tresses. "You almost died and I don't know how to be around you anymore. I did not want to get pregnant because I thought that what if he died and leave us alone, how was I going to bring up a child by myself? And it happened, you got shot and I almost lost you! Do you know how that makes me feel? I love you dammit! And I almost lost you!" Her voice had risen and then fell into a strangled sob.

He reached for her and she resisted at first, unconsciously thinking of his wound but then she dissolved into his arms, the sobs shaking her body. He held her and let her soak his t-shirt with her tears, his hands stroking her back, remorse and helpless anger roiling inside him. She moved away from him a little bit and looked up at him. "You did not want to get pregnant?" he asked her softly.

She looked at him guiltily. "No," she answered honestly. "I wanted to spend some time getting to know you better before a child came along."

"You should have told me," he accused her gently.

"You were so excited and I did not want to be the one to tell you that I did not want a child then," she whispered.

"Then?" His thick brows rose sharply. "Does that mean that you feel differently now?"

She took his hand and pressed it against her stomach. "I want this baby so much now that I have started eating lots of fruits and vegetables. I have even started drinking milk and you know how much I hate milk," she said with a grimace.

He laughed softly at the expression on her face and felt the emotion run through his body. "I appreciate the sacrifice," he told her teasingly.

"You had better," she told him in a threatening voice.

"I need my wife," he told her huskily.

"I am here."

"I need your body," he clarified.

"You are not strong enough," she protested.

He took her hand and guided her toward his crotch. He was as hard as a rock! "I have been without you for a week and two days, and I am not going another day without tasting you," he told her huskily.

"I don't want to hurt you," she moaned, her hand closing around him.

"You will only hurt me if you don't let me have you." His breathing was ragged as he rubbed her hand over his erection.

"I can't afford to hurt you that way," she told him softly. "But I will be doing most of the work, that's the condition."

"Deal," he murmured, his eyes narrowing as he watched her slip the soft cotton dress she had on. It was late afternoon and she had been to the store in the morning and came back home to be with him. She had not been wearing a bra and only had on black silk underwear that molded over her pubic area.

She released his erection and bending over him she took him inside her mouth, her tongue going over the tip of him before going as far down as his length would allow. He almost convulsed as her teeth grazed him slightly and he had to clench his fists inside the sheets as she continued to bathe him with her saliva. He moved his hips against her, his eyes closed and his body on fire with desire for her! She stopped suddenly and kneeled on the bed getting rid of her underwear before climbing on top of him. He guided his penis inside her and already wet with her saliva it glided in easily and her tightness closed around him causing him to take a sharp intake of breath. She sat still and he did not move either. She bent her head and took his lips with hers, their tongues meeting and delving. He held her hips and they started moving together, their mouths fused together, their bodies a combustible flame! He dragged his mouth from hers and eased her back a little bit, taking a stiff nipple inside his mouth. Kimberly felt the dart go straight through her and the combination of him inside her plus his mouth on her nipple had her almost bursting with intense need. She had almost lost him and to feel him inside her and now that he had been spared was so powerful an aphrodisiac that it almost destroyed her control. She buried her fingers into his thick dark hair and gave in to her desire, her body shivering against his. He shot his load deep inside her with a low feral cry, his body shuddering against hers helplessly. He had wanted to wait for her but his body decided otherwise. She followed behind him, her sobs echoing in the room, as she clung to him, calling his name over and over again!

*****

"I think Angela Katsumi Kamato and for a boy Peter John Kamato." She rested her head on his bare chest. They were both naked and he was running his hand lazily down her back, tingling her senses.

"Katsumi means victorious beauty," he murmured. "Are you sure about John?"

"Your father was who he was, Peter, but he was your father nonetheless," she told him seriously. "I want our son to have a part of his name."

"You are more generous than I am," he told her huskily, his hands tightening around her waist. "I love you, baby."

*****

Charles and Mitsui's wedding happened on a clear and sunny August afternoon at the same chapel that Peter and Kimberly had exchanged their vows. It was a small private ceremony and Mitsui looked gently beautiful in a peach organza dress that floated around her petite frame softly. Her wave of dark hair swung against her cheek each time she moved. Charles kept looking at his bride and beaming in his pearl grey suit.

"They looked so happy together," Karen said with a sniff as she turned to look at Debbie. Both Peter and Kimberly were their attendants and she was wearing a simple powder-blue dress that clung to her figure and outlined her generous breasts. Her husband could not take his eyes off her.

The reception was held at the house and the food was prepared by Gerard and was served underneath the gazebo near the poolside.

Peter stood up to make a toast. "Mother, I am happy for you and happy that you have found someone to spend the rest of your life with, someone who makes you laugh and who you can cry with." His gaze swung to his wife and he smiled at her tenderly, his gaze telling. "I have found that myself and would never exchange it for all the money in the world." He looked back at his mother and her husband and continued. "To both of you and many years of happiness." There was a cheer from the rest of the guests as they raised their glasses in a toast.

"How are you?" he murmured as he danced with her around the dance floor that had been erected. She rested her head on his shoulder and sighed.

"I am happy and in love with my husband. How about you?"

"Happy and in love with my beautiful wife," he murmured.

*****

"What do you think?" he asked her anxiously, holding her around her bulging waist. She was six months pregnant and two days ago the ultrasound had told them that they were having a son which had put him over the moon. He had taken two weeks from the office and had taken her to Tuscany where they had spent a week with Simone and her husband and he had used the private jet to take her to dinner in Paris and they had gone to the Bahamas for one weekend in December. He had decorated a huge Christmas with her and piled the gifts underneath the tree with most of it for her. Their house was almost finished and she gazed up at the towering stone and glass structure. He had not wanted her to see it until it was near completion. They were due to move in the second week of January. He had sold the house they were living in and the occupants were moving in soon.

"Isn't it a little too big?" she asked. Landscaping had started and there was going to be a garden at the front and one at the back. The swimming pool was already installed and there was even a porch swing and a tennis court and also a gazebo some distance away from the main building.

"You think six bedrooms, six bath, two living rooms, a dining room and two kitchens is too big?" he teased her.

"Peter," she protested.

"Okay, baby, but we are going to fill those bedrooms with kids aren't we?" he asked her huskily, turning her around to face him. She was wearing one of those very cute maternity dresses and a white cashmere jacket. Pregnancy had blossomed her and she looked more beautiful than ever.

"Is that so?" She arched her well-shaped brows at him.

"Maybe two more?' he asked her huskily, wrapping his arms around her.

"We will see." She stood on tip toe and kissed his lips softly. "Can you allow me to have our son first before thinking about other kids?"

"Absolutely." He kissed her back deeply and had her shivering more from desire than from the cold air around them.

*****

"You look so happy," Kimberly exclaimed hugging her mother-in-law. They had met for lunch in a café downtown. Charles had gone to get supplies for his piano classes he was having. He had extended the business at Mitsui's insistence, and they now offered adult and children lessons.

"So do you." She patted the girl's belly. "I am surprised your husband lets you out of his sight."

"He is at the office and told me he is coming home early," she said with a sigh, smiling her thanks as the waiter brought her a bowl of soup. It was the end of January and the cold was still lingering with snow coming down every other day. "We are having the house warming on Saturday and I want you to help me with the catering. Peter said I should just have family and friends over but I would also like to invite some of his employees and the board members. What do you think?"

"I think that's a good idea. I will make a list. How do you like the place so far?"

"It's lovely," Kimberly said with a sigh. "Huge but absolutely lovely and I also need help with decorating the nursery."

"Absolutely," the woman said beaming.

*****

"Brian, how about giving Mrs. Walters' kitten a little rub down to calm her somewhat?" Kimberly suggested. She had cut down on her hours at work, deciding to take her husband's advice to take it easy but she still came in for part of the day.

"Done, boss," he said with a salute and a smile.

She had argued about Peter because he wanted her to give up the store and stay at home. "It's not like you need the money, baby." His look had been pleading.

"I am not sitting home and twiddling my thumbs just because I am married to a billionaire," she had told him firmly.

"You don't have to twiddle your thumbs, you can finish decorating our home," he had said with a winning smile.

"I am going to leave that to the professional, thank you very much."

So they had arrived at a stalemate. She would come in for part of the day and leave early and get her rest.

Her phone rang just then and to her delight she saw that it was Simone! The week they had spent there had been so wonderful that they were planning to go back soon after she had the baby. Leonardo had treated them as if he had known them for a long time and had taken them on tours all over the place.

"How is my very pregnant friend?" she teased.

"Very uncomfortable and feel as if I am carrying around a bowling ball." Kimberly told her.

"Well I have news," she paused dramatically. "I am pregnant."

"Simone!" she exclaimed. "Oh girl, when did that happen?"

"Well let's see, the doctor said I am two months pregnant so I guess around the time you guys were here," she said with a smile in her voice.

"How does Leonardo feel?"

"He is on top of the world and annoying me with his constant hovering," she said indulgently. "I am so happy, Kim, that I keep pinching myself. We have found two very good ones."

"We have," she agreed softly. "Did Deidre tell you that she met someone?"

"She did and she is being very cautious but I think he is really into her and the best part about it is he has a job." They both laughed at that.

"I miss you, girl," Kimberly said with a sigh. She told her about the housewarming for Saturday and how she was going to be decorating the nursery.

"I really wish I was there." Simone sighed.

"Me too."

They chatted a few more minutes and then they hung up.

*****

She told Peter the news about Simone later when they were in bed. The large bedroom was mostly glass and stone and had a towering ceiling and a huge fireplace that had a roaring blaze going on. He had sold all the furniture and bought new ones that they had picked out themselves. The bed was on a raised dais and there was a delicate scroll work above the bed. The closet was huge and had two sections: one for her clothes and the other for his, She had teased him that his clothes were far more than hers.

"I am happy for them. Leonardo seems to be a decent hardworking guy." He was rubbing her belly with the cream she had bought to try and avoid stretch marks. He did it every night but was interrupted all the time because he would spread the lips of her vagina and take a taste which would lead to other things. He was fascinated with the bulge of her belly and was happy that she was not sick anymore but was eating everything in sight.

"I miss her so much, Peter, I wish she was here for the housewarming." She shivered as he opened her legs and dipped his fingers inside her.

"Can she travel?" he asked her huskily, watching as her lips parted and a moan escaped her as he rotated his fingers inside her.

"I think so." She was trembling. "Peter."

"Hmm." He bent his head and touched his tongue to her and she knew she was lost.

*****

The day of the house warming dawned bright and bitterly cold with snow falling rapidly, covering everything in sight.

All the staff had come over to work with them even though Kimberly had said that they did not need four household staff. "They have been with the family for years, baby, I can't just get rid of them." So they had stayed.

Her mother had come over and Deidre and Michael, her new guy, who was an accountant as well. Mitsui and Charles were in one of the bedrooms putting away their things because they were spending the night to help set up the nursery.

They were just about to sit down to dinner when the bell went. "I will get it," Peter told her before she could get up.

The house was filled with people from his office and there was also Brian who had brought his date with him, a buxom blonde that he said was the one.

"Where is the baby mama?" A familiar voice asked in the doorway. She could not believe her eyes. It was Simone and a smiling and darkly handsome Leandro behind her. She pushed back her chair and both girls met across the room, hugging each other tightly with Deidre joining them.

"Oh my gosh! How did you get here?" Kimberly asked holding her at arm's length. The girl was glowing. Her red hair piled on top of her head and the green winter coat lovely against her white skin.

"Thank your husband for that." She nodded in his direction. "He flew both of us here for the occasion."

Kimberly turned to look at her husband who was chatting with Leonardo and several of his employees. It was as if he felt her gaze on him because he looked up and caught her gaze. He smiled at her and nodded and she felt the love for him bursting inside her breasts.

They had fun and she broke away from the rest and took her best friends on a tour of the house. "How long are you staying?" she asked Simone.

"A week," she said linking her arms with her two best friends. "We are going to have so much fun!"

Chapter 14

The week flew by swiftly! Peter left them to their own devices only taking them out to dinner in some exotic and expensive restaurants along with Michael and Deidre.

Then the three girls went to lunch together. Leonardo was at the house by himself assuring them he was going to be watching television and cooking with Gerard as long as he did not mind him in the kitchen.

They went to their favorite café near the store. "I can't believe both of you are pregnant, I am starting to feel left out of this circle," Deidre complained sipping her hot chocolate. January was ending but the cold had intensified.

"You can always join us," Kimberly said teasingly.

"No thank you. Not until Michael puts a ring on this finger." She held out her left hand. "So tell us about Tuscany and living with Leonardo." She turned to Simone. Pregnancy made her white skin rosy, and even though she was not showing yet, she had a glow about her that was apparent.

"He is the kindest, most loving man I have ever known. Not that he compares to Peter," she said turning to Kimberly. "That man practically eats you up with his eyes and finds it hard to look at anyone but you, no matter who is in the room. But Leo is a gentle soul and he loves working with his hands. There are of course a lot of benefits with a man who loves to work with his hands," she said with a wink causing the other girls to laugh. "I do not miss home because where he is that's home and aside from missing you guys then that's it. We complete each other."

"That's so romantic," Deidre said with a sigh, resting her chin on her hands.

"What about you and Michael?" Kimberly asked her, automatically rubbing her belly.

"I am being cautious, you guys know my history when it comes to picking guys," she said with a roll of her eyes. "This time I am taking it slow, even though I think I am in love with him, I am prepared to wait."

"That sounds reasonable," Simone agreed. "Don't wait too long; you are not getting any younger." Deidre threw a piece of fry in her direction and Kimberly watched as Simone fielded it.

She had missed this, the three of them having lunch together and being together like this and she could not help but realize how much their lives were changing.

"Let's make a promise to each other," she said suddenly. "Even one time for the year we are going to meet up for a week to maintain our friendship. Either Simone, come back here or we go to her."

"Deal," the other two girls said in agreement, clinking their cups together.

*****

"How was lunch?" Peter asked her later that night. They had taken a shower together as soon as they had left Simone and Leonardo and gone up to their suite.

"It was very good." She told him about the agreement they had made to see one another each year.

"Sounds like a plan." He was toweling her off and paying special attention to her belly.

"How was work?" she asked him as he rubbed the soft towel on her belly.

"It was okay. Construction is under way for the new supermarket." He had stopped rubbing her down and bent down before her.

"Peter what are you doing?" she asked him faintly.

"Talking to my son," he murmured, tracing her belly. "PJ, this is your dad. I am so happy that you are going to be joining us soon to complete our family and I am going to be the best father you can ever hope for."

"You are calling our son PJ?" Kimberly's voice was tremulous. She combed her fingers through his thick dark hair.

"I am the only one allowed to call him that." He looked up her teasingly.

"I should hope so," she moaned. He had bent his head and had started licking her protruding mound. "Oh lord Peter." Her body felt weak.

"I need to pay attention to his mother as well." He dipped his tongue inside her and her legs buckled. He held onto her and his tongue thrust inside her over and over again until she was mindless with desire. He stopped long enough to get off his knees and lifted her into his arms, taking her into the bedroom to finish the task he had started.

*****

Teal blue was the color chosen for the nursery. Peter had had the wallpaper and furniture delivered and had asked her if she wanted a professional to do the job. "I have professionals," she had reminded him with a straight face. "There are Deidre and Simone and your mother as well as mine. We are planning a decorating party so don't come home too early."

"I am being banned from my own home?" he asked in mock distress.

"Just for a short time," she reassured him, kissing him lingeringly on the mouth. He had pulled her into his arms and deepened the kiss. They had ended up being late to get out of the house.

Karen switched on the button of the mobile and allowed the soothing music to fill the nursery. All the furniture had been put in place and the wall paper depicting monkeys and bears frolicking in a meadow had been hung. They had chosen the room not far from their own bedroom for the nursery and it was a large enough room with large windows all around to give the place light.

Both Leonardo and Gerard had prepared some delectable finger foods for them to enjoy while they decorated.

"It's such a peaceful room," Mitsui said with a sigh as she settled back against the cushions in one of the lounge chairs in the room. She looked happy and content and had started to put on some flesh on her petite frame. Kimberly could not believe that this was the same woman who had some months ago looked as if she was afraid of her shadow. Her cheeks had filled out and she looked serene and beautiful.

"How do you feel now, honey?" her mother asked her. She had brought over a large white stuffed bear she had found in one of the baby stores and it was perched along with the dozens of stuff toys on shelves in the room.

"Big and bloated and tired almost every day," Kimberly told her with a smile. "Peter says he wants more children and I want to tell him that when he grows a vagina and a uterus then he can dictate how many."

The others laughed. "Men!" Simone said with a shake of her head, her flaming red hair coming loose from the top knot she had secured. "Leonardo keeps telling me to let us go for another one as soon as I have this one so they could be company for each other. I look at him as if he has lost his mind."

"When I start having children, I want at least three," Deidre spoke up.

"Well, I suggest you start now, honey, because you are certainly not getting any younger," Simone told her dryly. She ducked as her friend threw a cushion in her direction.

The rest of the afternoon went by pleasantly and before they knew it, they were finished and it was time for those leaving to go. Deidre was spending the night because Simone was leaving the next day.

That night they sprawled in the large living room with a fire blazing in the hearth, eating chocolates and drinking nonalcoholic beverages and chatting until it was almost midnight. Both Leonardo and Peter had already gone off to bed.

*****

The goodbyes were tearful the next morning and the men stayed to one side as the friends made their tearful goodbyes. Peter had arranged a driver to take them to the airport where they would be travelling first class back to Tuscany.

"Thank you for a lovely time," Leonardo kissed both her cheeks softly. "We will look forward to see you when you both come by." He looked at Peter with a smile. "Thanks my friend." He clasped Peter's hand warmly.

"Take care of my girl," Simone told Peter, hugging him tightly before stepping back.

"Always," he murmured, pulling his wife into his arms. "Be safe."

*****

She felt such a feeling of melancholy hit her after they left that she had to go into the nursery to sit and look at all they had done. That was where Peter found her some minutes later. He had gone downstairs to check the alarm. It was a Saturday and he had stopped going into the office on Saturdays, spending the weekend with her. "Hey." He sat beside her and pulled her back against him. "I am here."

"I know." She burrowed into his strong embrace and inhaled his cologne and special scent. "I just miss her."

"And you can see her whenever you have a need. The company jet is at your disposal," he told her gently.

She lifted her head and looked at him. "You have changed everything in your life for me and sometimes I ask myself what have I done for this absolutely wonderful man I have? Whatever I have done is not enough."

"You have saved me from a loveless union and showed me that marrying for love was the only way a person can be happy." He framed her face. "I met you and my life changed for the better baby, so don't ever let me hear you say you have not done anything. You have done everything." His look was passionately tender.

"I love you Peter, my husband," she whispered.

"And I love you beyond anything I have ever experienced, Kimberly, my wife," he said huskily. That night he made sweet passionate love to her in their son's nursery, celebrating their love for each other.

*****

She was due on the third of April and as soon as the time drew near she started getting irritable and moody. She could not sleep well at nights because she was very uncomfortable and Peter would rub her belly and make sure she had enough pillows behind her head. She had stopped going into the store but made sure she kept on track with what was happening. She had hired a girl to help Brian and it was working out great. She had lunch with her mother-in-law and Charles at their house once a week and was taking piano lessons as well. It was a delight to see how happy they were together. Her mother stopped by two times for the week and was planning to come and spend some nights with them when she had the baby.

Her contractions started at two p.m. on the third of April. It had rained the night before and she had picked at her food at dinner and Peter had gotten concerned. He had held her in his arms for the night and rubbed her belly. He felt rather than heard her restless movements against him in the early hours of the morning. When a moan escaped her lips he was up like a shot. "Baby?" He switched on the bedside lamp and saw her biting her lip.

"I am calling the doctor." He reached for the phone and called Doctor McIntyre. He held the phone between his shoulder and ear and propped her up on the pillows. "She just had one," he was saying into the phone. "Five minutes apart?" He was watching her and saw when she stiffened. "She is having another one. I am taking her in." He ended the call and got off the bed, going into the closet to get something for her to wear.

His heart almost failed him when she called out to him. "Peter!" Her voice ended in a gasp as he hurried back into the room with a dress. He had called his mother and hers and they were going to meet them at the hospital. He saw to his consternation that her water had broken and he hurriedly got her cleaned up and slipped the dress over her head. "Breathe baby," he said urgently. He had already put some clothes on and he reached for her bag and a spring jacket that he put on her before heading out.

*****

Doctor McIntyre met them outside the hospital with a wheelchair. "Okay, Kimberly," she said with a kind smile. "Let's go get your son out."

She was taken into the labor ward immediately and a gown put on her. She was given something for the pain which was coming fast and furious. He put on a gown and sat at the edge of the bed, taking her hand in his. "You can do this, baby, I am right here," he told her softly. He had hated to see her in so much pain and had almost rear ended a car coming in the opposite direction when she had cried out at one point. Dammit! What had he done to her?

She nodded and squeezed his hand.

"The baby is crowning, Kimberly, so push only when I tell you to we want to avoid any tearing," Doctor McIntyre instructed her.

Their son was born at five a.m. weighing in at eight pounds two ounces and making his presence known the minute he came out. The nurse handed him to Peter as soon as she wrapped up in a blanket and he stared at the red scrunched up face in amazement. His dark hair so like his own was flattened against his skull and his dark brown eyes looked up at his father curiously. "I think he knows who I am," he said with a smile as he handed him to his exhausted mother.

"Of course he does," Kimberly said with an indulgent smile as she looked at her son. He was perfect and she could not believe that she had been having second thoughts about having him. She felt the love blossomed inside her as she stared at him. "He looks like you," she told her husband softly, looking up at him.

"I think he has your eyes." He kissed her lips tenderly,

"You are trying to make me feel better that our son looks like you and not me after I did all the work," she teased him.

"Caught," he said tenderly. "There is nothing I would not do for both of you." His voice was hoarse as he held her against him and gazed at his son.

*****

They had visitors bearing balloons and stuffed toys and flowers. Some of board members from his company and several employees came by to see the boss' son and of course both their mothers and Charles and Deidre were there.

Simone had called and told her she could not wait to see her godson. She was five months pregnant and said she looked like a trailer.

She spent two days in the hospital and then was told she could go home with her son. Peter came with a car seat and wheeled them out of the hospital, securing them inside the vehicle himself. He had not taken his driver with him, preferring to drive his family by himself.

Charles, Mitsui, Karen, and Deidre were at the house waiting for them when they got there and Gerard had prepared a tasty meal for them.

*****

"I really want one of them," Deidre murmured looking down at the sleeping infant. He was cozily dressed in a monkey suit with feet to keep him warm and a blanket thrown over him. His bottom was up in the air and his fists clenched beside his cheek. He looked so peaceful and contented. "He is going to be a heartbreaker when he grows up," she predicted.

"And I am never going to accept any woman he brings home to show me," Kimberly murmured, reaching out to touch her son's cheek lightly.

Mitsui and Karen stared at their grandson tearfully. Peter and Charles were downstairs leaving the women to fuss over the baby.

"I know I have no right to ask you this but I am just going to say it." Charles looked at the younger man steadily.

"You can ask me anything, Charles, you know that," Peter told him seriously. He felt closer to the man he had met in a little under a year than he had ever done with his own father.

"I never had kids," the man said sadly, looking down at the amber liquid in his glass. He and Peter were celebrating with age-old scotch. "I thought I did not mind but in fact I wanted children and I missed not having any. I would really like it if I can be an honorary grandfather to little Peter, that is if you don't mind," he added hastily.

"I would love that," Peter told him softly reaching out to clasp the man's hands vigorously. "My son could never ask for a better grandfather."

"Thank you, Peter," he said huskily.

Later that night when they got home and he told Mitsui, he clung to her and cried. His wife held him to her gently and her face was wreathed in a smile of satisfaction. She finally knew what it meant to have a family.

*****

Their son woke up in the middle of the night demanding to be fed in the most boisterous manner. Peter told her he would go and get him and carry him back to be fed from her breasts. He handed her some water to drink before she breastfed him and made sure she was comfortable while doing so.

"He is going to be very demanding," Peter whispered as he watched him latch onto his mother's breast greedily, his bright dark eyes unmoving.

"I wonder who he gets that from?" she asked him teasingly, wincing slightly as he pulled at her sore nipple.

"You okay?" Peter asked in concern.

"Just a little sore there," she told him with a smile. "The nurse told me it would get better as I continue to feed him."

He watched as she burped him when she was finished, rubbing his back and took him from her to hold him for a little bit until he fall asleep, before taking him back to the nursery.

"Hungry?" he asked her as he came back into the room.

"I am starving," she said with a laugh.

"How about I get you something to eat from the kitchen?"

"How about we both go and get something to eat?" she suggested, climbing off the bed.

"Okay." he took her hand and they headed downstairs to the kitchen. It was one of the largest rooms in the house apart from their bedroom and was ultra-modern with parquet floors, marble counter top and a circular island in the centre of the room. It gleamed in the dim light left on and they knew Gerard did not tolerate mess in his terrain. "How about a turkey sandwich with mayo and lettuce and tomato?" he asked, her standing in front of massive two door refrigerator.

"Sounds delicious." She climbed on one of the stools and sipped the Perrier while her husband deftly made sandwiches for both of them. He had on a loose sweatpants and white t-shirt and she could see the play of muscles in his arms as he sliced tomatoes. He looked up just then and caught her gaze.

"I love you," she told him softly.

"I love you too." he watched as she came off the stool and came towards him. He put aside the knife and opened his arms to her. "We have a son together and I cannot tell you how much that means to me," he told her huskily.

"I think I have a very good idea." She brought his head down and their lips met hungrily, their tongues meeting and delving into each other's mouth. "Baby," he groaned, pulling his mouth away from hers, his breathing ragged.

She surprised him by going down on her knees before him. "Kimberly?" he murmured as she pulled down his sweatpants and took out his semi-erect penis.

"I want to taste you," she told him and put him inside her mouth. He braced his hands against the counter and moved helplessly as she sucked him inside her mouth, her teeth grazing him slightly. She reached under to cup his testicles, squeezing slightly and causing him to shudder as the raging desire raced through him. She did not stop and it did not take him long to come inside her mouth, his body racked with helpless passion, his hands clenched on the counter as he flooded her mouth with his seed. She swallowed every drop of it and licked him dry until he thought he was going to die from it all. She did not get up until she had licked him clean and when she did he clung to her weakly, his body shivering against hers.

"What can I do for you?" he asked her hoarsely, his body still shaking. He could not believe the effect she had on him.

She pulled away a little bit and shrugged out of her robe. Her breasts were full and engorged with milk and the nipples large and stiff. "I need release."

"I thought they were tender," he said to her faintly, his heart thudding in his chest.

"I need this, Peter." She climbed on the stool and waited. He came between her legs and bending his head, he took a nipple inside his mouth pulling on it gently. Kimberly cried out sharply, her fingers clutching his thick dark hair as a bolt of lightning shot through her body! He used his tongue to soothe where his son had fed on and by the time he reached the other one she was trembling and clinging to him. He pulled her to the edge of the stool and taking out his penis, he rubbed it against her underwear. He was not able to enter her yet so he did the next best thing to ensure her release. She cried out against him and he took her lips with his, their bodies clinging together as the sparks flew between them!

Later that night after they had eaten, he held her close to him while they slept, confident in their amazing love for each other.

The end.

If you enjoyed this ebook and want me to keep writing more, please leave a review of it on the store where you bought it. By doing so you'll allow me more time to write these books for you as they'll get more exposure. So thank you. :)

Get Free Romance eBooks!

Hi there. As a special thank you for buying this book, for a limited time I want to send you some great ebooks completely **free of charge** directly to your email! You can get it by going to this page:

www.saucyromancebooks.com/physical

You can see a the cover of these books on the next page:

www.SaucyRomanceBooks.com/RomanceBooks

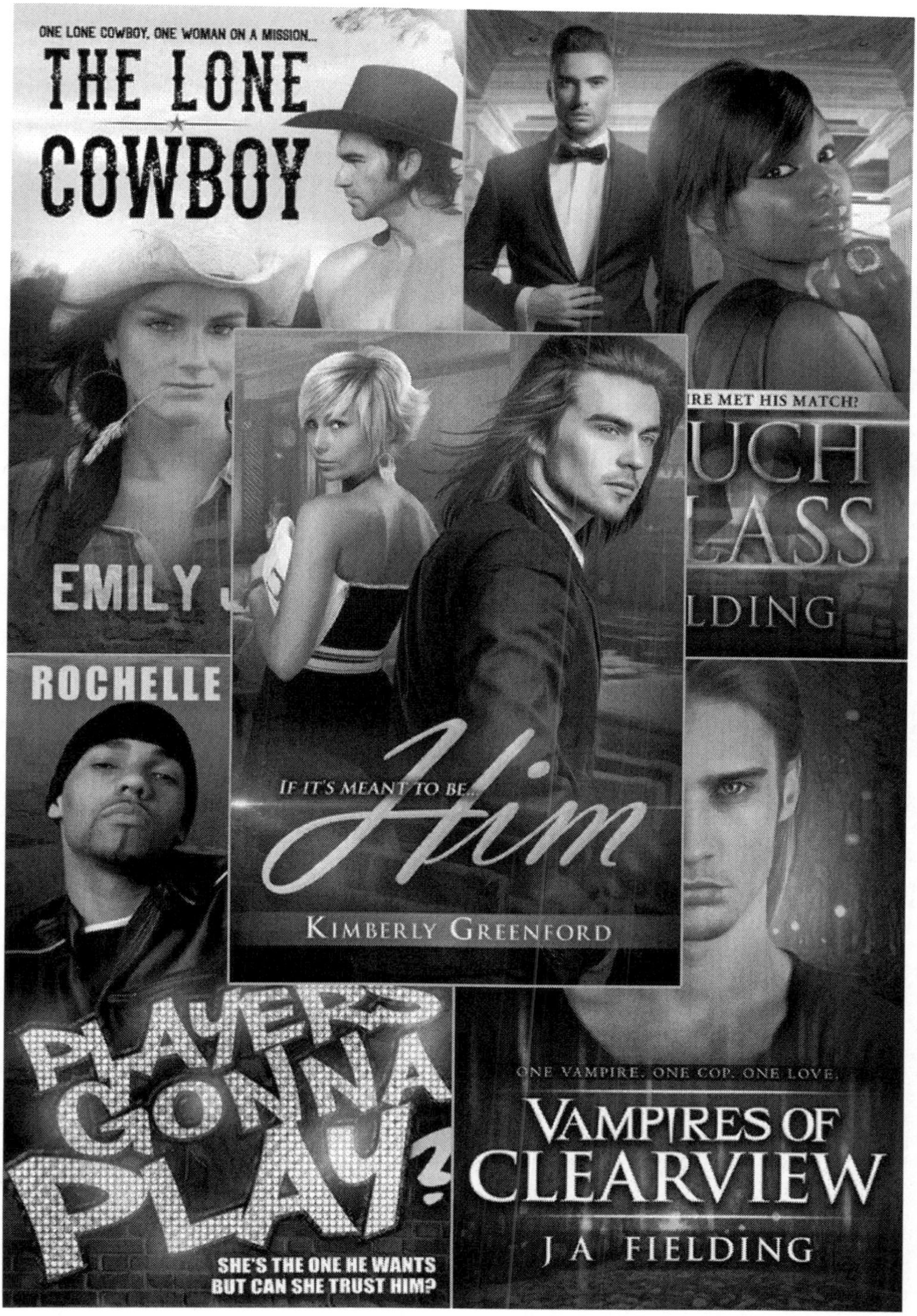

These ebooks are so exclusive you can't even buy them.
When you download them I'll also send you updates when
new books like this are available.

Again, that link is:

www.saucyromancebooks.com/physical

Now, if you enjoyed the book you just read, please leave a
positive review of it where you bought it (e.g. Amazon). It'll
help get it out there a lot more and mean I can continue writing
these books for you. So thank you. :)

More Books By Mary Peart

If you enjoyed that, you'll love Saving Her Billionaire by Mia
Cater (sample and description of what it's about below -
search 'Saving Her Billionaire by Mia Cater' on Amazon to get
it now).

www.SaucyRomanceBooks.com/RomanceBooks

Description:

Phoebe is a counselor who isn't sure she likes her job, and doesn't have a lot of luck in the dating department.

Nate, in contrast, has had an easy life - helped greatly by the fact he's the son of a billionaire and hasn't had to work for anything.

That is, until his father dies.

Not in a good frame of mind knowing that he has to take over his father's business, Nate goes to a bar to drown his sorrows.

It's there he meets Phoebe, and they end up going home together.

Nate thinks it will end there, but after falling further, he ends up at Phoebe's office as a patient.

It's there that he finds out Phoebe is pregnant with his child, and neither of them know what to do about it.

Will the two be able to make things work for themselves and their child?

Or will Phoebe have another name to add to her list of disappointing relationships?

Want to read more? Then search 'Saving Her Billionaire Mia Cater' on Amazon to get it now.

Also available: The Billionaire's Needed Surrogate by Gemma Augustine (search 'The Billionaire's Needed Surrogate Gemma Augustine' on Amazon to get it now).

Description:

Ramona loves her job as a nanny, but dreams of the day she can have a family of her own.

Charlie is a successful billionaire having a similar problem.

But as he can't find a woman to start a family with, he turns to surrogacy as a solution.

Through a series of unlikely circumstances, Ramona ends up being hired by the surrogacy agency and getting paired with Charlie.

Unexpected to both, the two meet and immediately hit it off.

They both know they've never met anyone like the other before, but vow to remain professional.

That is, until Ramona has trouble conceiving and the two of them decide to turn to more... traditional methods!

Will they be able to figure out the fate of their baby in a way that works for them both?

Or is one of them destined for heartbreak?

Want to read more? Then search 'The Billionaire's Needed Surrogate Gemma Augustine' on Amazon to get it now.

You can also see other related books by myself and other top romance authors at:

www.saucyromancebooks.com/romancebooks